"It's all there: eloquence, comedy, a childhood effectively captured, seriousness, an eccentric intelligence. *The Swan* delights."

WILLIAM O'ROURKE, author of
On Having a Heart Attack: A Medical Memoir

"The brilliant stutter-stepping and jump-cutting expertly mimic the mind of a ten-year-old, and the basic irony is stunning—that a verbally pyrotechnic book should be uttered by a mute boy."

MICHAEL MARTONE, editor of *Not Normal, Illinois: Peculiar Fictions from the Flyover* (IUP, 2009)

"Nothing short of dazzling."

LINDA NIEMANN, author of *Railroad Noir* (IUP, 2010)

"Lively, entertaining, funny, and often moving."

"*The Swan* is a story of childhood and a family's tenuous hold
on everything that once seemed solid to them. Jim Cohee's
lyrical and expertly crafted prose weaves a tale that is
enchanting, hilarious, heartbreaking, and uplifting. A young
boy's fantasies and his resistance to the circumstances of his
family weave this story of loss and the transcendence of the
human spirit. It reminds us how noble and resilient we can be."

the swan

break away books

the swan

JIM COHEE

INDIANA UNIVERSITY PRESS

Bloomington & Indianapolis

This book is a publication of

INDIANA UNIVERSITY PRESS
601 North Morton Street
Bloomington, Indiana 47404-3797 USA

iupress.indiana.edu

Telephone orders 800-842-6796
Fax orders 812-855-7931
Orders by e-mail iuporder@indiana.edu

*Manufactured in the
United States of America*

Library of Congress
Cataloging-in-Publication Data

Cohee, Jim.
The swan / Jim Cohee.
    p. cm. — (Break away books)
    ISBN 978-0-253-22343-2 (pbk : alk. paper) 1. Boys—Fiction. 2. Indianapolis (Ind.)—Fiction. I. Title.
    PS3603.O326S83 2011
    813'.6—dc22

                                2011004519

1 2 3 4 5   16 15 14 13 12 11

For

LINDA KAY SMITH

He will throw you like a ball into a wide land.

ISAIAH 22:18

ACKNOWLEDGMENTS

The author would like to thank the following for their generous help: Linda Oblack and Jamison Cockerham at Indiana University Press, Anne Scheele at Orchard School, Jon Cohee, Danny Moses, Merryl Sloane, Linda Kay Smith, and Mark Terry.

the swan

PART ONE

smedley

1

I ran the path around the swing set in the side yard, ran with
pinwheeling arms, my mind gone in dreams of baseball triumphs,
and I supplied the sound for my phantom radio, the exhilarated
play-by-play and, behind that, the intergalactic whisper of
amazed and joyful fans—a whisper, but huge. Pentecostal
frenzies gripped the stadium when I snapped fly balls out of the
air in right field and threw runners out at home. I also recoiled
from the blows of boxers while I ran, then counterpunched and
POW! I decked them and circled the ring with raised arms—my
manager wept—while thousands in darkened halls stood and
cheered.

I leapt from couch arms and crashed a million times bet
ter than anyone in the world. I could slide in stocking feet on
floors farther than anyone, and I could skate on the ice at Holcomb Gardens in tennis shoes and play hockey with a broom. I
could fold myself behind couches and under beds and never be
found.

I rescued people. I fell through a million bolts of cloth into
black space in dreams. I caught spies. I wrestled snakes. Drove
dog teams. Sailed rolling shark-infested seas on my log raft—

winds whined like electric motors in the shrouds. I shot leaping tigers out of black air at midnight while pitiful Indian villagers wept in fear. I persuaded a Greek goddess to rescue Christ while grasshoppers buzzed in Muncie cornfields.

I laughed at fate. I saved the world. I knew all about my double on another planet, whose name was Noraa Repooc.

After my little sister, Pookie, died in the car crash, I developed a weird astronomical theory about my family. They weren't mine—they were space-traveling actors.

I walked right to the edge of the White River, though my mother told me millions of little boys were buried there, drowned. I lowered myself on bridge piers to the landing and looked at cupped gray water. I talked to myself. Heard human voices in the hum of refrigerator motors and the ring of water pipes. Read messages in radio tower lights, whose imperturbable red pulse in Indiana night skies watched over all children and was wiser, more calming, and more kind than God.

I had two secret friends—protectors (though they slept when Pookie died) and spymasters invisible to my faux family—the ruined Hungarian count Blurtz Shemshoian and Blurtz's wonder dog, the miniature dachshund Nipper.

I stole ice cream from my brother, and he never knew.

The White River is channelized in Indianapolis, pokes along like sleepy pond scum in summer (bars of light fall on it, dragonflies dart across the light, zodiacs of yellow pollen drift through), flows south (the White) and west to the Wabash, Ohio, and Mississippi rivers, past Cairo Town, and on south by careened, rotted paddle wheelers and Louisiana moccasins to the Gulf, past Mexican oil derricks on the Atlantic filmy with yellow mist, past the mouth of the Amazon and short red Indians with painted faces and spears, 'round Cape Horn of leopard seals and penguins, then swings out west (the sea) like a chained hammer from the thrower's arms into the great Humboldt Current in the vast storm-tossed Pacific, runs with trade winds to palmy Polynesia, under the Southern Cross and squawky frigate birds to Indiana's sister isle, Tuamotu. (Hoosier and Polynesian are one there. "Buncha hooey" means "the four quadrants of the spiritual oneness" in Polynesian.)

The Creature was born in White River headwaters, in gloomy primeval swamps and corn bogs north of town. Around Muncie, I figured, where ancient pioneer Coopers are buried, who had once cleared forests, hunted bear, churned butter in wooden pails, built log churches and sang in them, and whose heirs now put up aluminum siding and drank beer and wiped sweat off their foreheads with red bandannas and grinned like crocodiles and sang "Whoo-eee!" The forests are now little copses on the horizon above a sea of corn. Swagged power poles guide you there.

I walked to the north porch of our house where my father sat in his white boxer shorts in the wicker chair by the Zenith radio (gray with a pitted speaker and gold spike that swept the dial like a clock hand). He tapped a Camel cigarette hard against his left thumbnail, then lit it with a paper match, shook the match out, and tossed it expertly into a large glass four-cornered tray. He exhaled from his nose and held the cigarette in his knuckled left hand by his cheek. His right hand robotically clapped and turned the matchbook on his leg. Beside him on the wicker table was a Schlitz beer can he had opened with a church key—two black triangular holes on the can top. He stared off. He scanned the yard and listened to Don Wells call a White Sox game on WCFL Chicago. White Sox misfortunes haunted my father's summer and made him moody. White Sox–Yankee games had a funereal weight to them.

He was slender with thick dark matted hair and dark beard stubble. He had jug ears like the farming folk he came from. Stalks and ears. His spine was slightly bent at the top, and it caused him to wince when he rose from his chair. He was pensive and had a knowing, unhappy face. His name was Major Cooper.

He was famous in our little house for his ability to add numbers—large numbers—quickly, which he did on command to amuse my brother, Mike, and me. He was skilled at card games and could not be defeated at gin rummy. He remembered the play, could figure out what you held, never gave you a useful card, and went down too fast. (We played crazy poker games too—spit in the ocean, baseball, low hole-card wild, deuces wild, everything wild.) Dad liked to read *Contract Bridge Complete* on the bus to work (he solved all the end-of-chapter problems, then started over), and he read bridge-tournament books with card-by-card scores. He read books on arthritis too (for cures) and books on his lawyer heroes, Abraham Lincoln and Clarence Darrow, defender of Eugene Debs and John T. Scopes.

Though a loner and scoffer, he nonetheless "for professional reasons" was treasurer of a fraternal organization called the Order of Moose. The Moose had prayer breakfasts, though my father didn't pray; created networks for businesspeople, which my father eagerly joined; and raised money for charitable purposes. The money was kept in a box labeled "Feed the Jesus Fund. God loves a cheerful giver."

He drove a Pontiac Star Chief.

A man of biblical powers, my father loved to sit on the pot and smoke Camels and read the newspaper. Hair grew out of his ears. Hair grew out of his nostrils. He could urinate for six days without stopping. He scowled at Mom when they were bridge partners. He hated it when she fanned her cards on the table and began to gossip. He'd say, "You had the nine of hearts. Why didn't you play it?"

My father started to go off script in the summer of 1957. He started to forget his part as a space-traveling actor, and I could tell when he inhaled on his cigarette, then blew two, three, four smoke rings and a long plume through them, I could tell he was light-years from me and was getting tired of his Earth job. Squirrels hopped across his view. Maple leaves swung and swished in the air before him. He looked through it all and heard nothing. He didn't want to play anyone's father or husband any more. He wanted to go back to his home planet.

2

I liked *Kukla, Fran, and Ollie,* a Sunday afternoon puppet show Mom and I watched on a TV console, a small, soft-shouldered wooden box about three feet tall with a convex screen. I liked Ollie, the one-toothed alligator, a prankster. I liked *The Honeymooners* Saturday nights, especially about mid-show when Jackie Gleason would make a fist at Audrey Meadows and say, "You're going to the moon, Alice," and she would fold her imperial arms and stare him down. (How beautiful she was, and how helpless he was before her—just as I would be. I saved Audrey Meadows from drowning a million times in dreams.) I liked *Wednesday Night Fights*. I sparred alone on my bed and defeated hundreds of boxing opponents—they never saw the punches coming and BOOM! they went down with lame arms and legs like wrecked windmills. I liked *Boston Blackie*—it wasn't on, alas, in 1957—a detective who wrestled criminals on the tops of apartment buildings. His head hung over the roof ledge. Then he threw them off and they died. And I liked *Ramar of the Jungle*. I packed tall frosted Tom Collins glasses with ice, poured RC Cola over it—the foam hissed—and curled up in the overstuffed chair to watch the guy walk into the quicksand on *Ramar*. He struggled to escape, but sank with hideous slowness inch by inch—flailing arms clutching at nothing. His head went down, then his hands. Then he was completely gone. His pith helmet floated on the mire. Amazing and wonderful. The most beautiful and truest television show ever made. Quicksand is how we all die! I dreamed about the pith helmet.

I dived hands-at-sides like a seal into bed at night and slipped under my ratty safety blanket, an old cotton-batting quilt that was coming apart but that I would not surrender. You had to be careful not to leave hands or feet hanging off the bed because the Creature might be hiding under there, and if he saw your foot he'd take it with webbed bloody claws.

9

My mother's favorite word was "refinement." Life's main task was to get refined. Mike and I got refinement lessons every day. Handling silverware. Posture. Greeting people. How not to make a fool of yourself in restaurants. The importance of religious observances. Dressing appropriately. How to be nice to old people. Deportment around teachers so they wouldn't completely hate you. How to introduce people. How not to ask goofy questions or prying ones. The ones you wanted to ask. ("Did you rob *everybody*?")

For me, Mom had a special class. She called it Life Class. She cornered me in the bedroom and delivered little human empowerment talks. She sometimes pulled out cards, which she read and showed me. Sometimes she tacked them to the wall. Her name was Celeste Cooper.

One day she said, "Look at me, Aaron. You are very brave. Look at me, sweetheart. Remember that. You are very brave. You are not afraid of life's rude surprises, and you can come to grips and move on and have the life you want to live, OK? You understand that . . . Aaron?" Her voice started to break there.

I nodded my head.

"We have to be brave," she said. "We are going to be brave, and I mean that, OK? I want you to say yes."

Mike, who was in high school and had a girlfriend—he wouldn't go to church any more, which Mom called unrefined—Mike said, "It's a bunch of crap. Forget it."

I scooped the ice cream for dessert for the family. I always gave myself a little more than I gave Mike. I figured that over the years that would add up to a few truckloads of ice cream. Sometime in the future, he would be in a hospital bed, really old and decrepit, his bony vibrating hands reaching to me as he told me how important my friendship and wisdom had always been to him, what a hero I was to him, how grateful he felt for my understanding and love. His unshaved mandible would start to quiver. That would be the time to say, "Sounds good to me. Let's talk about the ice cream."

3

My friend Dana was the Captain and first preceptor of the spy ring the Order of Rhinoceros. I was second preceptor and Exalted Horn. No one would ever find us. We had a secret sign. You stuck your lower jaw out and flashed your teeth. We met in Meeting Hall 2108, our garage. The Order received messages from the Department of Galactic Purification. Constellation shapes, origami ciphers, pings and static on the radio, winking doll eyes, message-bearing elm leaf shadows on clapboard at 2 AM—all were communications from headquarters.

Dana and I spied on people and betrayed them to the police. What they bought. Where they went. We followed them into grocery stores. We followed them when they walked home from work. (We followed Dad's secretary, Basha Usakowski, home from work several times. She got off the bus at Meridian and 16th.) We wrote suspicious conduct reports about them and mailed the reports to the local police station. We turned in everyone. New kids in the neighborhood. Teachers. Baseball coaches. Enemy of humanity Kong Warthead. Dogs of various varieties. Basha recently of tragic Poland with her little boy, Paul, and her dogs. Shy and curious and bug-eyed and slow to talk, like me, was pitiful Paul. (Mr. Usakowski was gone. Bluto Usakowski, whatever. Russian tank driver. "He got tired of her," Dad said.) Mrs. Usakowski was not an American. She spoke French. Mom also spoke French. Refinement. Basha was Polish. The Department informed us that she was a Communist spy. First clue: she didn't wear lipstick.

I published my poetry in various avant-garde literary journals in Finland. (*Chomi Chimi Chak Chung*, for instance— "Forest of the Eternal Fount.") Blurtz subscribed to *Chomi* and despite the use of my *nom de plume*, Neptune Ullapool, he knew the poems were mine. He *felt* they were mine. He would read them, fold the magazine in those bear mitts of his, and weep. He would talk to me at length about my poetry. "You have astringencies," would Count Shemshoian say, "and your poetry is the martyred atrocity of Western literature, if I may, sir, and also, I mean this humbly, druidical. Something humbly and vastly quercidical about the dissonance and the stuck-horn incivility of this leaf-like and compacted verbiage. Your theme is bane and revanche."

He had been reading from my first collection, *Rocky Ripple and Other Poems.*

> *O captain! my captain!*
> *O'er fruited plains of Evansville.*
> *Let all the world in every corner sing, Amen!*
> *If the right one don't get ya, the left one will.*

Oh, when he sat at my bedside! His right hand held a cigarette in the crotch of the first and middle fingers—his fingers held his chin when he drew on that cigarette, the red ash signaled to me—the orphic smoke coiling up. I loved his weathered head with all those teeth set like tombstones in his jaw, his herringbone jacket and vest, slacks of red silk, black patent leather shoes. He could turn his head like an owl, that's how wise he was. Turn it one hundred and eighty degrees with a jerk and study the floor SNAP! He felt things so deeply, he had experienced life so fully, he had tutored so many literary celebrities and had so thoroughly mastered Western civilization. ("Oh that little Bonobuonocottilucci"—my rival in Italy—"he would creep up and whine at my toes! But he could never write this, Mr. Aaron, sir.")

> *Bonobuonocottilucci,*
> *Married the daughter of Americus Vespucci.*
> *Got arrested for hootchy kootchy*
> *Way down in Egyptland.*

Dana and I had a cipher, Oweeyon, and a decoder ring.

Our favorite mark was Mrs. Schemler, who walked the neighborhood and looked at you furious and befuddled and (the Order of Rhinoceros found out) danced naked in her basement Wednesday nights with Negroes and drank whisky from jugs. Yet she braved every plate that fate threw at her, for her faith was like a wall, and fate's hopes and desires were dashed against her love of God, and she sang to the bats despite her timidity and lack of encouragement, "Oh yoi yo yuppa yo!" She was only sad, we learned later, after we imprisoned her for a million years.

"Dear Police Department. We saw suspicious conduct today from Mrs. Schemler at 419 Blue Ridge Road. She was sitting on her porch and snapped her fingers at us. Put her in jail. Bye. We do not live in Rocky Ripple. You will never guess who we are. Bye. Mr. X."

My favorite song was "Stranded in the Jungle" by the Cadets. "Stranded" is about a man who finds himself in a boiling pot in the African jungle; he seems to wake up there. He escapes and swims to America to search for his girlfriend in Lovers Lane, but in Lovers Lane another boyfriend is singing to her. The song's refrain, "Meanwhile, back in the jungle," became the refrain of our family. A taunt about non sequiturs and cluelessness. Dad's favorite song was "How High the Moon" by Les Paul and Mary Ford. Mike liked "Chances Are" by Johnny Mathis. He could dance close to his girlfriend, Linda Lavalliere, when "Chances Are" played at Shortridge High School dances. (She pronounced her name lava-leer.) Mom liked "Lisbon Antigua," a chirpy violin-and-orchestra piece. "Lisbon Antigua" says Europe is a sunny and happy place. When you hear it you want to skip across Portuguese cobblestones and embrace your girlfriend by the family yacht. I also liked "Heartbreak Hotel" by Elvis Presley. It's down at the end of Lonely Street. If you ever fall for somebody, you have to go there. And I liked Vaughn Monroe's "Ghost Riders in the Sky." Dead cowboys drive the devil's herd in high western clouds.

4

It was after Pookie died in the car crash that I became interested in the red light on the radio tower. I could see it from the cinder track at Butler University, and I would stand in the center of the field to gaze at it. The light said, "The world is good. You are safe here."

Mom showed me that, high in the summer sky, above the blinking light, I could always find the constellation Cygnus, the Swan. The wings were difficult to pick out at first, and so were the weak stars of the neck of the south-flying Swan. In the tail of the constellation was Deneb, a first-magnitude star. "That's where Pookie is," Mom said, "surrounded by horses, asleep with her little arms outstretched like a swan on the snows of Deneb."

And it was about this time that I began to acquire unusual powers. When I would go out rat hunting at night with my rat knife, for example, the next day the neighbors and all garbage men yielded to me. Schoolteachers bowed to me. Ministers asked me for understanding.

There was a strange silence when Pookie died, in every baseball stadium in the whole world.

Uncle Skipper said, "It's time for your facts-of-life talk, OK? Here we go. Let's just dive in here. Now there are some things women do that men cannot do that are pretty damn gruesome. Start right there. The worst of them is a thing called 'the horn circle.' With me, Aaron? Look at me. Their breasts—excuse me for using that term—their breasts are actually horns. You have to be careful how you squeeze those things because, you lose control in that situation, you lose your hearing. Take control of your impulses, first rule of adulthood."

I wondered if he had told this to Mike, and I thought of Linda's breasts. Those things were large enough to blow off lampshades.

"You see those old guys with hearing aids, you put two and two together. Now. Women honk at each other, little known fact. You have to adjust to that, and that's what adult life is about, adjustment. Aaron? Accommodation. You can't have everything. Stay calm. Women stand in a circle and honk at each other. They think it's God's plan, huh? They can't help it. It's instinct. It's a defense mechanism. You're walking by a house and you hear this kinda submarine honk-squawk kinda thing? Blurp-barrup . . . blurp-bap?"

I shrugged.

"And you're not sure where it's coming from? That's the horn circle."

Thursday afternoons I got out of school to see Dr. Epstein. I thought he must be four hundred years old. He was bald and there were weak little individual white hairs on the top of his head. He smiled all the time, the clown's smile. On his desk was a sign that read, "I am your friend."

"I am your friend," he said. "Do you believe that? Believe it, because it's true. I want to tell you a story. I have puppets, and it's the most amazing thing. Do you like puppets? Their names are Morrie and Reba. I talk to them, and they have their own world too, naturally. But you know what? You know what, Aaron? . . . Aaron? Listen to me. They talk to each other. Do you want to see them? I have them in a little box here. They are really very nice, and I know they would like you very much. Do you like puppets? You'll like them. They are going to be your friends."

He brought them out. They were both cloth hand puppets, like socks. One had a mustache and a cap whose top snapped onto the brim. He carried a pencil like a baseball bat. The other had a red wig and a red mouth. "This is Morrie . . . and this is Reba."

The puppets were suddenly animated, and they were thrilled when they saw me. Morrie said, "Hey, Reba? Reba! Look! Do you see that? It's Aaron!" In Dr. Epstein's left hand, Reba shook in the air. They were waving their arms wildly, and I waved weakly back with two fingers.

"Oh, they have their little fights now and then," Dr. Epstein said, "but look how happy they are to see you."

I liked the puppets. They whacked each other with the pencil once in a while. Morrie whacked Reba and she'd grab the pencil from him and whack him back. I enjoyed that. Every time they saw me, they went a little crazy with excitement and happiness. They were my own Kukla and Ollie, except they were in a box all week thinking about me. ("They have been asking about you, Aaron. They want to know what kind of week you had. They asked me just yesterday, 'Oh boy,' they said to me, 'Is Aaron OK? Can we talk with Aaron?'")

The intriguing thing was watching Dr. Epstein, watching him make the voices and work the hand puppets. Watching the muscles of his face pull at his compressed lips and his Adam's apple jump in his throat. He was even better than the puppets. He didn't look so old with them either. He didn't look like a clown. When he put the puppets in the box ("We have to say good-bye to them, now. Bye, Morrie. Bye, Reba. She's waving good-bye to you"), he looked happy.

5

My father's favorite writer was Charles Goren. He also liked Mickey Spillane and the Mike Hammer mysteries. In *Kiss Me, Deadly* Mike Hammer is flagged down by a woman wearing a raincoat. Under the raincoat she's not wearing anything. Hammer decides to help her.

Mom's favorite writer was Sara Teasdale. (Mom kept Sara Teasdale on a bookshelf built into the headboard of her bed. Beside the book was a drawer with condoms in it. I counted the condoms. She knew about it, because she would say, "Aaron? Look at me. Aaron? I mean it. Look right at me ... OK? ... Very important. Don't go in the drawer.") She also liked to use *The Complete Poetical Works of James Whitcomb Riley* as a book of divination.

Mike's favorite writer was Malcolm H. H. Chisholm, AIA, author of *How to Design Your Own Ranch House*. Mike drew ranch houses that had forty-two bedrooms, ten outbuildings, four hundred paddocks, an ostrich exercise area, a heliport, an expostulation chamber. He kept drawing them and redrawing them. "I want two pools," he said. "One shaped like a M, and one shaped like a C." He also liked *Mad* magazine. He'd stagger in the hall, holding the magazine in limp arms, looking like someone who had crawled through the desert and was too weak from laughing to ask for anything. He'd say, "Oh, man."

My favorite writer was Raymond L. Ditmars, author of *Strange Animals I Have Known*. Ditmars went to South America and pulled vipers out of bushes. Whacked pythons in India. Shot Brazilian tapirs if they got too close. Mapped the plate patterns of venomous snakes. Wrestled cobras in boxcars.

My favorite thing to do Saturday afternoon: scoop three scoops of strawberry ice cream into the blue bowl, read Ditmars, and think about expeditions to capture venomous snakes. My faithful guide would say, "He's over here, sahib." Then I'd march over and ZAP! You have to grab it by the head. I also liked Jack London's *Call of the Wild*. Abducted California dog pulls sleds in the snowy Klondike, escapes, and runs with the wolves. And Thor Heyerdahl's *Kon-Tiki*. The good Ahab sails his balsa-log raft four thousand miles from Peru to the Tuamotu Islands in the South Pacific. And Jim Corbett's *Man-Eaters of Kumaon*. Brave British imperial officer sits alone at midnight with his rifle across his knees in a tiger trap in the Himalayan jungle while villagers cringe. I loved Corbett. I also hunted tigers.

Then there were the books Mom asked me to read. *The Power of Positive Thinking* by Norman Vincent Peale. Mind cure and Jesus renew the troubled life. Warbled hymns. Mom was urging me to practice self-confidence, and I looked with a squint at the triumphant stories of *The Power*. To gain ground in the world, one must stride, apparently. Mom also recommended titles from the Classics Club, linen-bound books with titles gilt-stamped on red bands. *Nature and Other Essays* by Ralph Waldo Emerson, *Five Dialogues* by Plato, Thoreau's *Walden,* Francis Bacon's *New Atlantis,* Henry George's *Progress and Poverty,* Turgenev's *Fathers and Sons.* But I wasn't interested in Thoreau's bean rows or anything else in those books. Thoreau never shot a tiger. Reading a book to better the mind is a tragic idea. I knew what I wanted in books. I was headed for the bison and wolverine studies of Ernest Thompson Seton and for the best expeditionary book any boy could ever hope for, Leonard Clark's *The Rivers Ran East.* Clark hiked into the Amazon basin looking for the Seven Cities of Gold, and he found them.

The book business was important at home because Mom wrote short stories. Part of Life Class was Library Class. Mom wanted to talk about the books she loved, and she wanted me to love them too. She recommended writers who had the scope (she called it) to sympathize with women. (Like Thoreau, I guess. Socrates.) This capability was rare, she thought. Women themselves, mysteriously, had it. Jane Austen, Edith Wharton, Simone de Beauvoir. But also Leo Tolstoy, Noël Coward, Tennessee Williams. Mom also wanted to try out story ideas on me, ideas sympathetic to the experience of women, ideas she would submit to the editors of *Collier's, Redbook, Ladies' Home Jour-*

nal, and other fiction-publishing magazines for women. Keeping faith with her Celtic heritage (her maiden name was Ferguson), Mom wrote under the *nom de plume* Luna Dundee.

I wanted some kind of unnamable romance with a neighbor of mine—for I was as yet a knight errant without love entanglements—the rare and radiant maiden Margery Doebereiner, thirteen, mistress of my thoughts, long of leg, who rode in white pajamas through summer nights on her bicycle. (I fell through her clothing in dreams.) Margery had a girl's bike with the dippy crossbar. Balloon tires. One speed. White fenders. Weird, except it carried her. (Boys' bikes had horizontal crossbars, boys removed the fenders.) I had streamers (plastic strips, fillets, holy air crinklers) on my bike handles, and I also rode at night.

Margery had once asked me to take care of her pet hamster, Gog a good start. The hamster died, unfortunately. I sent her a note. "Gog is dead."

"Why did Gog die?" she said. Tough question. What kills a hamster? Heart attack? I didn't know. Infected toenail? Maybe it wanted to write poetry, came across a few lines of Shelley, and took its own life. Maybe, after two or three turns on the treadmill, Gog was unable to visualize success. Or maybe it got some bad hamster news and just conked out.

I buried Gog under the swing set, but Margery made me dig it up again. It wasn't there. Her neck began to swell, and she hissed at me. I had to put a noose around her and hold her off with a metal pole.

Dana said, "She's a snot."

I read the Sunday comics. Dick Tracy's chin was sharp as a finch's beak, and he burst into robbers' hideouts, pistol drawn, and said, "You're under arrest, you dirty rats." His enemies were like diseased vegetables: Flattop, Agatha Egghead, the Clipso brothers. Tracy called headquarters on a wristwatch radio.

I liked Arthurian knight Prince Valiant who rode anonymously in the lists before court ladies and knocked his enemies from their horses with ribboned lances. ("Who is that mysterious knight?" "Prince of Thule!") Pavilions roofed in white canvas. Pennants unwinding in summer air. Medieval magnificence under puffy cumulus clouds. The air of art is clearer than air.

And I liked the tough old seadog, Popeye, whose fat forearms grew strong with spinach and who struck back at the bully Bluto when Bluto made passes at skinny Olive Oyl. Popeye knew love and was brave. "I yam what I yam," he said. And that's what God said too.

Dana and I went to the bus stop at 16th and Meridian. Basha got off there and turned west. She had to cross the White River. Walk by the South Grove Golf Course. Walk to Medford and turn north there to 2011. It was pretty easy to follow her. You watched her get off the bus and then you bent down and followed along. As she walked, she would tilt her head to one side, and then the other, pulling off her earrings. Her purse hung from her shoulder, and she'd drop the earrings into her purse.

Mom and Dad had the Menards over for bridge. It was torture for Dad, who hated them both. He especially hated Mrs. Menard, who giggled and forgot the game. Mrs. Menard was a short fat python. She had a detachable lower jaw and could swallow people. She'd open up a little bit on the left side, then the right side. It took a while.

When Mrs. Menard laughed, her face shook, her breasts shook, her fat arms shook, her chin fell to her chest, and she put her bridge cards on the table in little giggle frenzies. Dad hated this. He hated it when hands were put down. He folded his cards into a neat little stack, crossed his arms on his chest, and gave Mom a hateful look. Mom put her hand down, fanned out, and smiled at Mrs. Menard.

"Tell Major about your sister Sylvia," Mom said. Dad looked at the ceiling lamp. "The one about the cat toy."

Mrs. Menard started to shake again. "Oh, that would take a long time," she said.

Dad paced the kitchen later, when Mom was at the sink and the Menards were gone. He said, "Stupid bitch."

The toaster began to slide down the counter, cupboard doors swung open, the curtains puffed back, then CRASH! the wave hit the window and glass blew in like shrapnel. Dad lost his footing and the refrigerator rocked. The gray hide of the shark banged hugely against the kitchen door. The ceiling light blinked.

A glass bowl fell from Mom's hand and broke on the tile floor. It rocked there, ticking.

Mom said, "Go to your room, Aaron."

"Dear Police Department. There is a missing cat from 303 West 44th Street. Its name is Chuckie. It is gray with dark stripes and has green eyes. I think Mrs. Menard swallowed it. When you stretch her out, where the bulge is, there's the cat. You will never find out who we are. Mr. X. P.S. Don't let her coil around you. Grab her by the head."

6

Dana said when you die you are dead for all eternity. How long is eternity? Dana said if the outermost tip of the primary feather of a little baby bird just barely touches an iron ball the size of the moon once every four hundred and seventeen years, when the ball is pulverized, eternity hasn't even started.

When you die you smell like poop, he says.

Down the block on West 44th Street was my classmate and archenemy Kong Warthead. His mother's name was Mrs. Warthead. It was difficult for Kong to walk because of the size of his butt. His legs were like giant plastic bags stuffed with marshmallows. When he moved, sinkholes opened in the street and cars rolled into them along with kids in baby carriages. Mothers screamed. Kong had soft round shoulders and his arms hung like gorilla arms. He didn't have hands, but links of chain hung from his sleeves.

When he walked, he had to heave one huge bossy leg around the post of the other. He went, "Huhn . . . huhn." He would wrestle me to the ground. When I got up, he would wrestle me down again. He'd say, "Why don't you even talk, huh? Hey, Aaron.

Say something. Hey, dumbbell." That was his only idea. That's all he ever said.

Mike brought Linda Lavalliere over. She got breathy around me. She weighed a hundred pounds, minimum. I was her special project, she said, and she thought how cute I was every day. (Mike said, "She basically says this about every ten-year-old guy in the world. Ignore it.") She put her hand on my head and her chest started to heave. "This one's going to be a hearrrt . . . brrreaker," she said. Her laughter boomed. The lamps shook. But as it happened, she had nothing on me because I had discovered the great secret of her romance with Mike (Mom would never know this). Mike got two fingers of his right hand under Linda Lavalliere's left bra strap recently. "She's stacked," he said, but unfortunately she would slap his hand away when he pushed it into the cup of her bra. She said, "Stop it!"

You have to get to the nipple, the Everest of that particular sport. A thousand climbers lay frozen dead on the last pitch. There's no way to get to the nipple. It's the ideal that can never be realized. Man cannot be perfected. So they fall with a shout from the cliff face, splattering ice from the ledges like shotgun blasts, then down again into crevasses—open shark jaws— where they freeze for a million years until outer-space creatures melt the ice and look down on them and they start to revive and they whisper, "I was only two inches . . ." Then they die.

Mike said, "A girl's nipple, if you ever see one, Aaron? It's like the tip of a hydrogen bomb."

Anyway, Mike couldn't get there. He turned back.

When Linda Lavalliere sat on the couch, I studied her chest and the bra material embossed on the white panels of her shirt. It was difficult to know what lay behind the buckled plackets there. Bird nests? Torpedoes? I also studied her scaly and unbeautiful knees. She crossed her legs, folded her hands in her lap, and said to Mike, "I'm burning my candle at both ends." (I thought, "Good luck lighting the bottom part.") Mike said he was thinking about going into professional fiction and thoroughbreds.

One more thing about her. Mom pulled me aside once when Linda Lavalliere was there and said girls Linda Lavalliere's age get electrocuted once in a while. For health purposes, girls had to take bat balm, cormorant egg whites, *secret de framboise*, and smashed crab eyes.

"That's something you need to know when you're ten, Aaron. Menstruation. Very important." She raised her finger. You had to look at her when she did this. "Be considerate."

I was pretty sure Linda Lavalliere was going to take Mike down to the end of Lonely Street. She did.

"Dear Police Department. Kong Warthead is loose in the streets again. Arrest him. Mr. X. You will need a decoder ring for the next letter. P.S. Linda Lavalliere eats slugs (pretty sure, not positive)."

Dana knew everything there was to know about Linda Lavalliere. Her father died of a finger trap, though nobody wants to talk about it because of the shame involved. If you push opposing fingers into a tube of woven straw, the straw closes and locks on your fingers when you try to pull them out again. Mr. Lavalliere foolishly pushed his first fingers into the tube one day when he was talking to Mrs. Blentlinger. He said, "Now you want to think about the international fungibility liquidity, because the dead hand of mortmain grips our extended limbs each and every day."

Mrs. Blentlinger said, "You are so fascinating sometimes."

Mr. Lavalliere's face turned with a rapt, dynamic immobility above his tireless elbows. "Because of constrepsit contamination transfers."

She noticed that his teeth were filed like sharp little pickets, and that saliva had wetted his chin, and yet she knew somehow, she wasn't sure how, that he wanted to penetrate her aloneness. Mr. Lavalliere and Mrs. Blentlinger stared at one another with long piercing looks, looks that descended unimpeded through their bottomless souls and into the final secret place where for an instant Mr. Lavalliere and Mrs. Blentlinger crouched flagrant and fearless in all the old panic and prognostication, bald, blatant, and unabashed. The lines of fate went off. Some went up. Some went sideways.

Mr. Lavalliere said, "Get the halo effect." Slowly he'd been pushing his fingers into the trap—now, suddenly and horribly, "Wait a minute, I can't get my fingers . . . Aghhh!"

Mrs. Blentlinger said, "Here! Let me . . ."

She fell on him. They rolled on the carpet. Puff balls rose. Her skirt came up. He died there, screaming on the office floor. The secretary ran in. Mrs. Blentlinger said, "He's a goner."

They had to bury him with the finger trap. People crowded against the casket rail to see his hands at the mortuary. He seemed to be asleep there, with a little American flag folded into a triangle in the corner of the casket. He wore a suit. In the straw tube, two fingers pointed to each other across Mr. Lavalliere's chest. Biddies in snoods went up to the casket and looked down on his fingers and said, "Oh, my Lord! Good gracious! Whaaa!"

Dana said, "Swear to God."

Linda Lavalliere said, "If you ever want to talk with me, I'll talk with you. I mean it. Aaron? Don't be afraid of me, OK? Call me if you want to. I'll talk with you."

On Saturdays I played Little League baseball at Orchard School on 43rd Street. I played right field for the Comets. There were too many players on my team so Mr. Amoroso, the manager, put out five right fielders, including Dana and me. Right field was basically a roped-off area for the blind.

Mr. Amoroso's hair came out from under his baseball cap like boreal shrubbery. He waddled around and pulled his pants up. He went to the mound to talk to Bobby after six walks. He said, "Bob? Can I call you Bob?"

Bobby shrugged.

"Does your Dad run the florist shop down there on Madison?"

Bobby turned an ankle and looked at his cleated shoe.

"You haven't thrown any strikes here for a coupla days."

Bobby looked toward third base.

"How do you feel, Bob?"

Bobby said, "Good."

Mr. Amoroso said, "Well, that's good enough for me."

My batting average was zero. I had not been able to get a ball out of the infield yet—or even into the infield.

I liked to catch fly balls when I lobbed them up for myself, or field grounders when I threw tennis balls against the garage door, but I didn't like to play at Orchard School in Little League. No privacy. Baseball without privacy is half a game.

Mr. Amoroso said, "Aaron, I want you to start thinking about your performance level."

Once when I was in right field, villagers came by torchlight to ask me to kill the Chowgarh tiger that had carried off a young maiden while she was gathering sticks in the field, and so I went on a brief sojourn to that stricken land, for there is no more terrible thing than to be under the shadow of a man-eater. I followed the trail down a steep hill through bracken and ringals with my rifle alone. The girl's mother, I was told, had ceased to speak when she found her daughter dead. I set out at once, for it was a many-days journey to Chowgarh.

Pookie was my cheering section in the old days. She would bring a little metal trumpet to the games, a street find, and whenever I went to the plate, with every pitch, and with every attempt in the field, she'd blow on the trumpet.

The ball kicked off my foot. I chased it down and threw to second base. The runner slid in safe.

"I will kill the tiger," I said, "and the woman will speak."

"Dear Police Department. You will find suspicious conduct at 6106 Nimitz Drive. Mr. Amoroso lives there. In his backyard he trains tomatoes on strings that hang from wooden poles. He sits in a white Adirondack chair and drinks red wine from jars and looks at the tomatoes and doesn't say anything. His hair flies out all over the place. Bye. Mr. X."

7

Mom said, "Or this one: young man named Denby Winton, a college student, one day near the end of college, while sitting alone, suddenly sees a young coed. Her name is Maria Kolisch. She catches his glance. It seems so meaningful to each of them, their love so destined somehow, and yet, by a quirk of fate, they never really know each other. She taunts him with her beautiful eyes. He writes poetry for her. ('Who is Maria? What is she? / Sitting in rondure all up in a tree. / O lady of th' umbrageous grot, / Who is Maria? What is she not?') They tragically just go on with their lives, as people do. They lose touch with each other. Winton makes a bright career for himself as a copywriter for a big advertising firm in Chicago. Everything he writes dazzles everybody, but he is secretly wretched. Something's missing. Then, one day, in a train station in Cleveland—he's there almost by accident—while he's having a cup of coffee, entertaining the people around him with his brilliant jokes and causing general mirth in the train station, he sees Maria Kolisch at a nearby table. He stops talking and gazes at her, and she returns his gaze. She is dressed in a gown, with pearls looped over the front of her dress. She is wearing furs; there are ten peacock feathers in her hat. She looks at Winton and remembers suddenly that she loves him. The feathers sway under the ceiling fan. The rivulet of a single tear finds the corner of her mouth. Beside her sits a geezer with disheveled hair and droopy eyelids. His palsied right arm is thrown over the back of her chair. His head jabs at the air while he coughs his tubercular cough. Eight fingers are heavy with jeweled rings, big as bosses. One of his eyes falls on the table and he has to palm it back in. He says, 'Oh! B'Jesus, Gawd! Haw! Aghgh! 'Scuse me, now, uhmnn.' The Glance."

Mike played catcher for the Shortridge High School baseball team. I'd seen him tag people out at the plate. He could also throw his mask off and catch foul balls. There were some things I didn't like about Mike, but I also liked some things. One was when he said, "If anybody ever hits you, Aaron, tell me about it and I will beat the crap out of 'im." Up to that point, nobody had though, or even tried to. The other was what he was with his friends on the team. He'd get in Eddy's car and ride to the Rendezvous, a hamburger joint on 52nd Street, across from the cinder track at Butler. They'd order a Doctor Death, a cherry Coke with a straw that had a skull on it. They laughed hard with each other, and they had extraordinary powers. One was going to Princeton to study mathematics. One built a radio station for Shortridge High School, and it actually worked. They moved with unbelievable efficiency through the world, I thought. They were gods.

Once every million Saturday nights, Mike would knock on my bedroom door and say, "Hey, power hitter, let's go." I'd get in the back seat, passenger side, of Eddy's car—Eddy, the pitcher—and we'd go to the Rendezvous. They'd turn on the radio and listen to Jimmie Rodgers sing "Kisses Sweeter than Wine," and the Everly Brothers, "Bye Bye Love." They ignored me, but they were also like my private army. I drank the Coke and watched the light on the radio tower. I listened to their jokes and to the music. With them, it was like rocking in the bucket at the top of the Ferris wheel.

One more thing I liked about Mike. When he walked with Linda Lavalliere—they held hands with locked fingers—he was the emperor of Shortridge High School.

I always had the same thing for breakfast, Quaker Oats with milk and sugar in the blue bowl. A deed to one square inch of the Yukon came in the Quaker Oats box. I owned six square inches. I would one day own the Yukon and drive dog teams into Russia. They'd be sorry.

I was eating my cereal at the kitchen table. Dad was sitting across from me, drinking coffee and smoking. Mom came in the kitchen door with milk bottles in her arms. She had picked them up from the milk box that was sided with a metal that looked like tin foil. When she was angry with Dad, she wouldn't talk to him, so after she put the milk away, she left the kitchen. He told me a story.

He had a client, a man named Turfy Knolls, who had borrowed money to start a business. The client wasn't able to repay the money on the terms of the loan agreement, and the lenders had come after him. He came to Dad to ask for relief. Knolls needed six months more, he said, to get the business going to where he could start to make the loan payments. If he had to liquidate assets to repay the loan now, the business would fail. Could Dad keep the creditors at bay? Dad tried to put them off, and the case went to court. The judge sided with the creditors.

The case tortured Dad. He talked about it and paced through rooms thinking about it, sometimes at night. Mom would go downstairs in her nightgown and say, "Major, come to bed." He paced and smoked.

It upset him, he said, that his client lost his business, and it upset him that he had actually put a small amount of money into the business himself. "Small," he said. "Don't tell your mother. When an attorney does his job right, you don't go to litigation. The idea is to stay out of court. You talk to people, calm them down, find a way." That didn't work this time. It also upset him, he said, because the attorney for the plaintiff was Mr. Menard.

I went to the Little Church of Christ Methodist. Dad wouldn't go. Mom went and seemed to fall asleep there. Mike wouldn't go unless Linda Lavalliere went. I went to the youth ministry in the basement. There was a chalky light down there, and the rooms were like dream chambers.

You were delivered into brutish hands in those rooms, into the hands of youth minister Geoffrey Felsing, my movie star. Geoffrey had a tattoo of the weeping Christ on his left shoulder, which he showed me once in a while, and he would tell me about his crimes. Once, he beat up his girlfriend. Once, he stabbed somebody. He had also robbed Vonnegut Hardware. Two policemen had come to arrest him, and he told them he would not be arrested. He had violent opinions about Negroes and would pick fights with them. "Blessed is the one against whom the Lord will not reckon sin," said Geoffrey Felsing. Now, he ran the youth ministry. (God knew everything about him but liked him anyway.)

Mom said everyone needed a moral frame of reference, and the church provided that.

Geoffrey Felsing was built like a wrestler. He had short-cropped hair, a big chest, and strong hands. When this meatball took you by the shoulders, you felt yourself pulled by metal grips. He said, "You will find your voice in Christ, Aaron."

He had been angry at everybody because his father was mean to him. Now, he wasn't angry. He had found Jesus and was calmed.

He would tell me about the police chases and the prison brawls, but all of his stories had one ending. "Jesus died for you. Do you know what that means?"

He'd pace his little office with an open Bible in one hand. I was supposed to know why Jesus died. It was a blood-of-the-lamb thing. The dead lamb, the sacrificial lamb, saved us all somehow, though I couldn't figure out how killing a little lamb would save anything. Doesn't anybody care about the lamb? But when Geoffrey got excited and started to shout, it was better to lay low, better not to answer. He could look at people with eager eyes, the eyes of Blurtz's wonder dog, Nipper. "It means God loves every . . . single . . . person on this planet."

One Sunday he said, "Today, we have a special invitation to join our parents in the chapel, and I want everyone to line up at the door, and we are going to go very . . . quietly—Do you all hear me?—very quietly upstairs."

"Hooves roared the ground trembled horses flew across the ground. The morning sky lit up the track, but one of the fastest horses was Wonder. She was a chestnut with a star on her forehead and a sock on her left front foot, other than that she was reddish brown. Her jockey's name was Johoyah Crimson."

That's Pookie's story, "A Horse Called Wonder." Not bad for a seven-year-old. She loved horses and she loved writing stories about horses, and she was going to live in Montana one day, buy a ranch, buy a horse named Rocket, she said, and ride it all the time.

She had a little horse library. Books by Will James—*Smoky, The Drifting Cowboy, My First Horse*—with their pen-and-ink drawings of bucking horses and of cowboys leaning against corral fences.

She was also the greatest scavenger ever. She was the little mouse in the field that was searching, searching, searching all the time, and she would come home with all kinds of weird stuff. She had a coin changer that, when she clipped it on her jeans, gave her a professional air. She'd march into my room with the changer and say, "That'll be a nickel." She made Dad fill the barrels, and she could make change fast. In time, it became the most precious thing I owned (after Ditmars, after my bike, after *Call of the Wild* and *Kon-Tiki* and *Man-Eaters of Kumaon*). The metal was polished like a mirror and the mechanism worked perfectly. I clipped it on my belt the way Pookie did, and I learned to make change fast too, and I had a big feeling about it. The changer was my amulet against harm, and there's a little story there.

Once, when I had been dreaming and waving my arms, but away from the safety of the swing set, I walked into a street sign and fell and felt stupid and was crying and couldn't figure out why. Pookie said, "I don't see what's so bad about it." What's so bad about waving my arms and talking like a radio and looking crazy to the world. And going off and not coming back when other people would come back. She gave me the coin changer.

It was hard being strange to my family, even if they were from outer space and really weren't mine. But later, without Pookie, I knew it was going to be harder.

Anyway, I got Pookie's books (*My Friend Flicka, Black Beauty,* the James books, *The Yearling*—about a deer, actually—*Misty of Chincoteague*). I got Pookie's doll, naked with ratted hair, the horse postcards, and the plastic horses: trotters (whose fey prancing legs were ridiculous and still are), Arabian stallions (statuesque, storybook horses), shaggy fat hoofed Clydesdales (heavy and stupid and lonesome—I wondered how many sleds they could pull), thoroughbreds with jockeys in silks and riding helmets, unicorns. I didn't even like horses.

And Mom gave me Pookie's baton, a metal tube with a large white rubber bulb pushed onto one end and a smaller white nib at the other. My magic wand.

People from all over the world called me and asked how to write a poem. I didn't tell them though.

8

Dad's favorite movie was *Guys and Dolls*. Mobster Sky Masterson falls for someone at the Save-a-Soul Mission. Mom's favorite was *The Trouble with Harry*. She liked John Forsythe, who played a painter courting a young widow. Forsythe reminded her of someone in college who had written poems to her. Mike's favorite was *The High and the Mighty*. Pilot John Wayne, shaky and with a troubled past, lands the damaged airplane and saves everybody. The newlyweds in the back of the plane get panicky and touch each other. Mike studied this. My favorite was *Creature from the Black Lagoon*. The Creature kills people and abducts the scientist's girlfriend. The girlfriend faints, and the Creature carries her in webbed claws to his cave and lays her out, unconscious, on a stone slab.

The Creature peered at me from behind the cracked closet door at night. When my eyes closed, he sneaked under the bed. He waited there—he didn't sleep—waited there for my foot to hang over. (He was afraid of Nipper though.)

I was the venerable venator of West 44th Street, and I had spent a good deal of my infancy attacking rats with knives. When

I was two, my father had given me a Martini-Henry rifle—dead accurate up to any range. I knew how to hunt. Prowling bears and leaping panthers were my stock in trade at the time. I could track game at midnight through any terrain. The neighbors gave me plenty of respect, believe me. A sensible though suppressed sensation passed through the helpless ones when I walked among them.

Dana told me Basha Usakowski was a Communist spy and would have to go to jail. So we took the bus to the Circle, a traffic circle in the middle of town with an obelisk, a war monument, ringed by office buildings. Dad was on the thirteenth floor of one of them. We took the elevator up with the intention of sneaking around Basha's office, eavesdropping on her, and turning her in.

Basha was blonde and slender and plain. She pulled her hair severely back. She spoke quickly, nervously, and seemed to know what you were going to say before you got there, and she answered instantly when you stopped talking. She spoke French with Mom once in a while. She lived, Dad said, "very simply" with Paul, her infant son, and with her dogs.

Basha said we could not sneak into Dad's office because Mr. Knolls was in there.

Dana told her that Dad was a Communist.

Basha said, "You have no idea."

I ran the path around the swing set in the side yard. I was driving the sled behind a team of huskies high above the snowy timberline in the sad and lonely north. Buck—primordial beast in dog fur, matchless in strength and savagery and cunning—Buck led the team. Snowdrifts were hundreds of feet deep here, and avalanches cracked and echoed like battery fire and fell in cascades above us. I had lost Dave. Spent and weary from the treacheries of the north, weak in the traces, Dave had been dying a slow and terrible death. Exhausted. Whimpering with lost pride. No confidence. Helpless. Couldn't pull any more because of bad paws. I had to shoot old Dave. Then I called out to Buck, "Mush, Buck! Get on there!" and on we went.

An unkindness of ravens strutted up to Dave and pecked at his eyes. He was dead though. He didn't move.

Poor sick Margery, wrapped in blankets, lay in the sled.

I looked up from the bed and saw a complicated pattern of light on the ceiling. The light coasted along the wall like a sled. I heard the strange tidal flow of cars in the night street, the click of tappets and the whine of car motors (car motors are unhappy), and saw the pulse of turn-indicator lights on the ceiling. While the Creature was planning to attack me, the lights swept down the wall and disappeared.

I got up. I looked at the closet to see if the door was ajar. The Creature was in back of that door. He couldn't attack me now. The door was closed.

I tiptoed downstairs to the kitchen and took two frozen Christmas butter cookies from a bag in the freezer. The cookies were star shaped, made with a cookie cutter, sprinkled with red sugar beads and white confectioner's sugar. Mom had kept them in the freezer six months. I filled a glass jar with water from the tap and took two gulps. I put the jar down, snapped a cookie, put it on the counter, then walked to the drying rack. I touched each dish and counted them all. Six large dishes. Four salad dishes. One bowl. I put the other cookie on a plate and walked it upstairs. Dad was snoring. (There's a secret message in snoring, but no one but Mom knows what it is. Mom said, "I will one day give you a snoring grammar.") I put the dish on my desk and dove into bed. I dreamed I was falling through Margery's clothes, and my arms shook a little, and I said, "Oh!"

The Creature stalked out of the closet. Poison dripped from his horrible fangs, his breath caught in his throat, his claws pained him and troubled the air. He took some of the red sugar beads, crept back into the closet, and closed the door.

The electric football game. The players buzzed backward into their own end zones and fell over. The cap gun and the narrow red roll of paper caps that curled above the hammer. The black holster with silver studs. "What parta Indunaplus are you at?" The mechanical monkey, banging cymbals with its stiff arms. *Catcher in the Rye.* "Jesus Wants You for a Sunbeam." Pineapple upside-down cake. Buddy Holly. The foot-over-foot lunge of the slinky down the carpeted stairs. Ricky Nelson. Pick-up sticks. View-Master. Wooly worm. "He's puttin' on the dog." Rosemary Clooney. Dick Tiger. The plucked chicken doll (limp and raw, with red splotches). *Boys' Life.* (On the cover, laughing boys in Boy Scout uniforms drove tent pegs with hammers. They were too happy, I thought.) "For cripe's sake!" The green GI Joe soldiers I pushed across the desk while bullets ricocheted off the ceiling. Cotton candy like spun clouds on tall, narrow paper cones. Jack Lemmon in *Mister Roberts.* The rubbery vomit toy. "Hell's bells." ("It doesn't matter. Who cares?") The globe of gumballs. Parcheesi. Daisy chain. Canasta. "Revoltin' developments." Lincoln logs. Funny bone. Old Golds. Tail fins. Pete Seeger. Autherine Lucy. Dusty Rhodes. Crystal radio. Hannah Arendt. Pat Boone. The smell of new-mown grass. The pet alligator that died in the bathtub. ("You have to give it some water, Aaron. You can't just let a baby alligator walk around an empty bathtub.") *Auntie Mame.* Formica counters with scored metal edging. The letter from the wild-pets store in Florida. "Mr. Cooper, I'm sorry, It is against the law to put a king cobra in the mail." Mom's green beans with cream of onion soup baked in a casserole dish and topped with cornflakes. *Cat on a Hot Tin Roof.* Annette Funicello. The stuffed iguana Uncle Skipper gave me. "Get a buzz on." Lilacs hanging like grape clusters. Hollyhocks like flowering spears. (Name three beautiful things. The stem of the morning glory twined on the stoop rail. The script on the Coca-Cola sign illuminated at night. The moth that lights on the lamp with wings outspread, wings like marbled paper.) Wilma Rudolph. Edie Adams. Singing cowboy Jack Buck. "Watch your manners." Muriel cigars. The seat-cushion fart. Kewpie dolls. Bumper cars. *Paths of Glory.* Polliwogs. Christmas seals. Black Volkswagen bugs. "Dope fiend." The smell of talc on the barber's brush. The sound of bowling balls smacking pins (detonated gourds). Sam Levenson. Doilies. Fish fry. Mr. Bluster. "Duck and cover." Pale tiddly winks (pale pink, pale blue, white). Gray globe of dandelion seeds. Stools like pedestals with red Naugahyde disks for cushions. Bop City. Water-balloon grenades. Gisele MacKenzie. Flash Gordon. Mom's white chenille bathrobe. "Cracked 'iz knuckles." The restaurant booth's Sebring 100 Wall-O-Matic jukebox with pronged pages and nacreous keyboard (dime a song, three for a quarter). *Atlas Shrugged.* Dave Garroway. Erector set. "Shit on a shingle." The spikes and dull nubs of jacks. (I could never master bouncing the ball and scooping up the jacks—one more jack with each throw. I could, however, spin jacks.) *The Strange Career of Jim Crow.* Gene Fullmer. Watching one praying mantis devour the head of another—the wages of sex. Peeling foil off TV dinners. "Have you lost all sense of decency?" Gorgeous George. Firefly lanterns. (Mayonnaise jars with fireflies in them—fireflies caught with cupped hands. Mom would punch holes in the lid with heavy sewing scissors. "They have to breathe, Aaron.") Popping tubular legs into brackets on the bottom of the TV trays. Jimmy Durante walking upstage across pools of light. "Good night, Mrs. Calabash." (I wonder about her.) Smith Brothers cough drops (wild cherry). Beulah the witch. (When you say you're not well, she says, "That's nice.") The back-lit roller blind, watermarked like somebody peed on it. (And the swinging cord below the hem, and the twine-wrapped pull.) Revere Ware. Palm-hammering the bottom of the ketchup bottle. "Is there something you'd like to share?" Tired blood. Burma-Shave. Midges milling under porch lights at night. Sons of the Pioneers. "Takes all kinds of people to make a world." Kilgore. "Don't speak to me in that tone of voice." Zippo lighter with the hinged top. (Its flint wheel and torch flame. When you snap it closed, you have power.) Robert Frank. Jitterbug. Heavy balloon-tire Schwinn bikes. (Indestructible. You rode them and threw them down.) *A Face in the Crowd.* James Agee. *Peyton Place.* "I'm Buster Brown. I live in a shoe." The dopey Danish tables with spike legs and copper ferules. "He's swishy." (Walks like a woman. He's queer.) Twin popsicle sticks, blond, down which purple cricks forked and forked again on mortal wrists. The toy spring-loaded jaws that clacked on the tabletop. Pleated paper cups. The fat-bellied Minute Minder on the stove. Stan Freberg's "John and Marsha." Negroes with glassy marcelled hair. (The way teenage Negro boys shaved parts in their hair. Life's about hair!) The kilnmouth heat of noon at midsummer. The incredible weight of summer air. "Cowabunga." The cigarette and the bow tie of Garry Moore. The strawberry shortcake Mom made: pie-crust rubble tossed into a bowl with strawberries and drowned in milk and sugar. "You don't like girls, but just wait." Clouds that sat like pashas in the sky and would not move. Steam rising from heavy, granular cornbread (baked in a square casserole dish). "Seven ways from Sunday." (Every which way.) The staple on the nose of the balsa-wood glider, and the red Air Force star on its wing. (Not properly balanced, the gliders dove to the carpet like bricks.) Baloney with French's mustard smeared on white, spongy Wonder Bread (an Indianapolis company), which "helps build strong bodies eight ways." (And even more ways later.) The balloons on the Wonder Bread package. Green Jell-O with amber pear chunks on a bed of iceberg lettuce. (Pears from Tuamotu.) Radio Flyer wagon. "Icebox." Pedal car. Starlight Theater. Girls in winter coats with mittens clipped to coat sleeves. Black boots with metal clasps. Knit caps with lynx ears. Those girls had smoky breath. Kroger's. Green Stamps. Milkshakes in fluted glasses with long-handled spoons. The paper sleeve of the straw—blow dart! Jack Kerouac's *On the Road*. "Say goodnight,

Gracie." Hungarian Revolution. Green hourglass Coke bottles. (A shapely girl was said to have a figure like a Coke bottle. Linda Lavalliere had one of those.) You pried the cork out from under the bottle cap, I can't remember why. Bob Gutowski. "Tell ya what I'm gonna do!" *Andrea Doria*. Judy Holliday. "Socked 'im in the jaw." Wringer washer. *Queen for a Day*. The secret life of underwear. "Aaron Cooper Wins World Series of Right Fielders. A shy yet magnificent boy with vision difficulties rose from his wheelchair yesterday at Victory Field . . ." The braided lath of the clothes hamper, white with a black lid. Marlon Brando. *The Cisco Kid*. The metal Band-Aid box. (We are saved by the tiny red thread on the paper sleeve of the Band-Aid.) The jar of marbled grease on the stove. "All arooni." The chalked hopscotch grid on the sidewalk. (Nine squares. You hopped one-footed and two to retrieve the bead-chain lager, and you had to pick up the lager before your foot touched down on its square—a girl's game.) Art Carney. "Bitchin'." Pulling chicken pot pie from the oven with pot-holder mittens, then stabbing the crust with a fork to let the steam out. (That steam had mystical import. It proved God. I gazed at the steam.) Mechanical arms stretching saltwater taffy. *Tea and Sympathy*. The fanged car grill, cars with fins, cars shaped like fossilized fish. Styrofoam dice hanging from rearview mirrors. Say fast, seven times, "She sells sea shells by the seashore." *Sheena, Queen of the Jungle*. The falsetto of Andy Devine. "Fussbudget." The party hat that is a paper cone with elastic chin strap. At the peak of the cone, a bent pipe cleaner. Newsreel. Wham-O! Toffee apples. The horn of Clarabell. Ollie's tooth. The fortune-telling Magic 8-Ball. Candy corn. The megaphone sound of the television speaker. *Lolita.* (Kerouac and Nabokov passing in cars at night in western Nebraska.) The tongue of the noisemaker. The smell of hot red cinnamon on toast. *Victory at Sea.* The cartoon cat on television whose jaw dropped to the floor; its eyes rocked on springs in front of its face. "Wherever you are." The match-head bomb.

9

Mom snapped beans over the sink and cried. She said, "You have to have courage, Aaron." And when I cried, she called me to her, put her wet hand on my shoulder, and said, "I will only say this a million times, OK? Stop listening to me"—she kissed my forehead—"because even the best of couples quarrel sometimes."

The satraps and prefects sat in perfected traps.

Cooper spelled backward is Repooc. My name spelled backward is Noraa Repooc, which is the name of my double on another planet. A darkling changeling duckling. He doesn't make mistakes. Repooc is a Serbian word meaning either "king of slugs" or "spark of light on the mystic lake." Mom says, "Hey, Mr. Repooc, you have to be nice to Mr. Amoroso. His wife died."

The critical thing about dinner was to keep all the food groups separate on the plate. Thousands of children died all over the world every day when gravy seeped into their green beans and poisoned them. Kids ate the beans and threw back their heads, mouths open, and died in their chairs instantly. Got rigor mortis and no one could move them and they had to be carried off like Pompeii ash dummies. There was nothing you could do. There's no anti-venom for green beans mixed with gravy. So foods that touched were instantly inedible.

Mom said, "Aaron, it won't hurt anything. They're fine."

I looked down at my plate. A tarn of gravy had burst through a wall of mashed potatoes.

"Sweetheart, I'll put the beans on a separate plate."

Small green flames flared on the dish, then raced across the field of dead beans. Black smoke rose. Flies death-dived against the table.

"I'll put them in a cup. Give me your plate."

Crabs began to crawl across the bean flames.

Mike said, "Cut the crap, you little twerp."

"Aaron, sweetheart. Look at me. Your food is fine."

Once, I vomited at the table and Mike and Mom and Dad were washed into the street on a flood of half-digested tomato sauce and meatballs. Mom went, "Awk! Gagh! I can't swim, Aaron! Gowp!" I gave them the Order of Rhinoceros sign.

I had a fish in the freezer that Dad caught in Lake Shafer. It was dead, but it came back to life like Jesus when I took it out and pushed it around the water in the plastic swimming pool. Then I put it back in the freezer.

Dana said once a burglar was in Mrs. Menard's bedroom going through her diamonds and everything. Her pseudopodia crept up under his pants cuffs and she got the suckers going. The thief went, "Uh-oh." Then she snapped her beak and bit his butt repeatedly.

In summer I would visit my grandparents in Martinsville for a couple of weeks. My grandmother was stocky and rocked on pained feet when she walked. My grandfather was narrow and tall, a deeply reserved and pious man. I sat on the screened-in porch in the white wicker chair and watched Arthur Godfrey on television. He sipped tea and said, "Umm, that's good." The McGuire Sisters sang "The Naughty Lady of Shady Lane." I studied the hooked rug before me. Its pale threads were thick as cobras.

Mrs. Blankenship would come over. She must have been at least sixty. She always baked a cake when I came to Martinsville. Devil's food cake—chocolate cake with chocolate icing. People have died trying to shoot this into their veins. She'd walk over, carrying the cake with two hands, and my grandmother would call me to her and run her fingers through my hair the way Mom did and burble, "He's such a sweet boy," and Mrs. Blankenship, who had no children, would churr like a parakeet, "Don't I know?"

Uncle Skipper said, "D'I ever tell you the one about Smedley Never Returned? Hmn? Heard this one when I was prospecting for uranium in Uruguay. Geological survey in Uruguay. Ready? Here goes. Smedley was an anaconda hunter in Brazil, traveling with a team of snake and spider specialists along about 1948. They're all decked out in their safari jackets and everything, with the tents and suitcases of scientific vials, and microscopes, and pistols. They're in Brazil. They're in the Amazon. You have to go armed in there. The jungles of Brazil, according to the National Geographic Society, are just this side of unbelievable, Aaron. The Society has lost thousands and thousands of explorers in there. Peccaries eat 'em. Those animals have shifty and Peruvian ways. They come charging in from their hiding places and clamp down on explorers' kneecaps and give them a shake that like to put them out of their misery right there . . . You don't believe me . . . You are a half-second from moon dust, one of those peccaries get ahold of you, and I mean by that that when you die in Brazil you are on the far side of necrotized, boy. You are stone-cold dead with one of those peccaries on your knee . . . They eat ten-year-old boys mostly, peccaries Like to gnaw on 'em . . . It's evolution, Aaron. They have adapted to their habitat.

"Now, the jungles of Brazil are *thick,* and I mean so thick that when you try to walk through them all kinds of twigs and vines grab at you, orchids and everything. Spiders come flying down to attack your ears—they go in your ears, lay eggs in there, and when the baby spiders hatch they eat your brains out. Whaddya think? You don't have any brains after that. You won't be solving any arithmetic problems when those spiders get in there. The mother spider crawls into the right ear, and the baby spiders crawl out the left down there in the Southern Hemisphere. You might think about getting a hearing aid for that side if you ever go down there. They're called brain spiders. *Spidero cerebro macerando.*

"Oh Lord, honeysuckle vines of a Brazilian variety grab your fingers and saw 'em off. Monkeys howl atcha.

"Anyway, ol' Smedley, he's walking down the jungle trail looking for anacondas, not hurtin' anybody. He's got his hands in his pockets. He's wearing his new jungle duds. He's an Englishman. He's whistling 'An Old Friend of Mine'—a beautiful tune that will bring tears to your eyes when it's whistled properly. And what happens? Huh? What happens to Smedley? He comes to a fork in the road! And what does he do there? Think about that for a minute. What exactly? Is he going to take to the right side or the left side?

"He takes the left side. You were going to say that. I can read your mind, Aaron. You were thinking 'left side.'

"When I look into your thoughts I worry, because you do have thoughts in there that no ten-year-old should have now. Your dear mother will never know. Those thoughts would break her heart—don't even try to deny that—but naturally that's just between you and me, and I'm willing, if it means that much to you, I am willing to deliver sworn affidavits and writs and motions and file them, Aaron, in a safe deposit box in Uribe del Tosta Mondial down Mexico way should anything transpire in some goddam judicial proceeding requiring you to surrender your thoughts, which in some countries that hate freedom and liberty is quite possible, like this one.

"Smedley walks on. He shouldn'a gone in there alone, that's the first thing. Ol' Smedley was a slow thinker on this particular day, and he got tired as everybody does walking through jungles, very tired. Poor Smedley couldn't hardly keep his eyes open, now, he's really tired. He can barely plonk one poor little boot . . . two inches or so . . . his new boots, explorer's boots . . . all polished. And what happens? Huh? He sees a log lying across the trail, and he sits down on it. He sits down on the log.

"He takes his hat off. He wipes the sweat off his forehead. He folds his arms. He crosses his poor tired ol' legs. He's starin' off. The little butterflies are flutterin' around. He looks up and sees the soft green undersides of the leaves in the forest canopy, and he smiles, the world is such a beautiful place, it's a miracle. It *is* a miracle, Aaron. Ol' Smedley, now, he's looking up under the skirts of the forest and thinking about his beautiful girlfriend, Opal, as any man would do in that situation, when WHAM!

"Oh my God. The monkeys howl and fly. Leaves and also leaf fragments of various proportions come floating down. Forty-five feet of fangs and murderous coils have struck ol' Smedley and Smedley disappears in the coils . . . He had sat down on a anaconda! . . . Oh! And he's gone now. I hate to say that to you because of your tender age, but in one-tenth of a second ol' Smedley disappears in those huge merciless coils and that anaconda starts to squeezin' on him and squeezin' and before long he's as flat as a bath mat. He is so flat, Aaron, that you could not even recognize ol' Smedley at this particular stage."

Three flying saucers cut across the sky behind the elm trees on Sycamore.

"All right, now, what happens? Those howler monkeys, they're headed for Ecuador. They're scrambling across trees like scared parakeets. They don't want any part of that anaconda.

"Dust balls rise on mountain peaks two miles away when that fierce animal strikes. A high-energy wave of energy moves out from Smedley's crushed nasal passages at that particular instant.

"Now, back at the camp, Opal is sipping champagne in a flute in the tent. She's got her sights on Leslie Leopold at this particular time, and Leslie—Leslie's an egg-sucking, squinty-eyed, commie-queer intellectual—Leslie looks down and sees the champagne start to rock in his flute on the table, and he says to Opal, 'An anaconda has struck in the woods.'

"There was a terrible silence at the table now, because where is Smedley? He's *in* the woods.

"Oh, they searched and they searched and they searched some more, but they never found poor Smedley. And that was a sorry camp for a while, because Smedley never returned."

Mr. Amoroso and Mrs. Menard stole condoms out of Mom's headboard drawer and threw them at each other naked during a Comets baseball game and had to be arrested. Mrs. Menard said, "I can do all things through Him who strengthens me."

I ran the path around the swing set in the side yard. My balsa-log raft listed and righted itself fifteen thousand feet above black Pacific Ocean ravines. In the soft swells, the logs, pulling against the ropes, rose and fell like piano keys. The parrot screamed, "Bad boy! Bad boy!" Margery stood on the high yard, nailing the ham radio antenna to the masthead. On deck, squids snapped at me with sly and evil beaks, and their tentacles were devilish and ductile.

A million fathoms below the moon, I held tight to the steering oar.

My faithful companion Ambjorg . . . but where was Ambjorg now? I pulled his shrunken head out of my back pocket and gave it a quizzical look. Scorpions the size of lobsters had attacked him when he was whacking away at balsa logs in the Peruvian jungle. Ants the size of alligators had gnawed on his toes. Sinister Peruvian cannibals had boiled his head down to the size of an orange and sold him in a Lima flea market. He looked unhappy at that size, but I knew in my heart that Ambjorg wasn't really there any more. He was in Tiki-world now, smiling down on us each day the sun shined. For his sake, I had to sail on. No matter the danger to me and Margery, for we were born to danger.

The yard creaked and swung around a few degrees. The sail flagged, then filled. A soft Pacific breeze lifted my hair. Sharks vicious and huge, completely at the mercy of their emotions, circled the raft with open mouths.

Linda went to a party, sat on the kitchen table, and gave a kiss to anyone who asked. Eddy asked for one. Mike got mad at her. Now Mike won't talk to Linda. Linda said, "Oh, you big baby!"

At Dr. Epstein's one day, Reba took the pencil from Morrie and gave him a whack. "I want to sleep in a separate box," she said. Morrie shouted, "No!" Reba said, "Yes!" Morrie said, "No!" Reba said, "Yes, yes, Mr. Morrie, hunky dory. And you know what? Huh? You know what, Morrie?" Morrie said, "What? Go ahead. Say it, Reba! Jeez!" Reba said, "You didn't like the prawns!" Morrie said, "That's a complete fabrication. I did not say I didn't like the prawns!" Reba said, "Had it up to here, Morrie." Morrie said, "Those prawns weren't so bad. I mean, they weren't terrible . . ." Now Reba opened her red bird mouth and turned to Morrie. She said, "And you know where you can put your career." Morrie said, "All right. That's enough. I have had just about enough!" Reba said, "No, you haven't! You haven't had even *near* enough. It's your fault!" Morrie said, "Now calm down, Reba." Reba said, "After a while, baby doll." Morrie said, "You are not leaving." Reba said, "You *bet* I'm leaving. I am gone. You know gone?" Morrie said, "You are not leaving, Reba. Come back to Earth for ten minutes and let's . . ." Reba said, "Yeah, well who's going to stop me? Huh? Tell me that." Morrie said, "Can't we just, like two . . ."

It ended there. I don't know why. The muscles in his hands gave way. The puppets fell into a kind of coma. They drifted down to the desk, and he pulled his hands from their shirts.

Dr. Epstein said, "What have we learned from this experience today? We need to talk about our problems. Do you see that, Aaron? That's the point. Morrie said some rude things to Reba, and she's getting back now. She's getting even. Morrie needs to say he's sorry, that's all it is. They need to talk to each other and smooth things out."

There was silence. We looked at each other. "Do you want to play chess?" he said. He set up the pieces painfully. He gave himself the first move, but then lost his knight right away and shrugged and tipped his king over on the board. "And that's it," he said.

Blurtz Shemshoian came to my bedroom door, creaked it open, and leaned in. A flash of lightning illuminated the scene. The shadow of Nipper's tail wagged on the floor. Blurtz Shemshoian's face was gray, heavy in the lower part, with protruding teeth. His jaw was the size of a keyboard. In his gap teeth were intimations of joy and the knowledge of God, and his eyes had a corpse-like humility. (For I had sewn the brain of Gog into the skull of Blurtz Shemshoian.) Massive gray hands hung lame at his sides. Grave-worms crawled in the folds of his flannel and—Oh!—black buffalo bats jerked from his shoulders and circled the ceiling and horror-howled inaudibly. Blurtz would never reclaim the throne now. We both knew that.

I said, "Blurtz?"

Blurtz Shemshoian said, "The hound has bit off the Lady Rowena's leg, sir . . ."

Two cats screamed.

". . . which is now a vast and trunkless leg."

Nipper came in on quick stiff legs and sniffed the air. His nails clicked on the floor, and his small yellow eyes burned with a vicious light. He was constantly in motion, and I knew that a dog of Nipper's power could charge through walls. Nipper, in fact, was the only thing in the world the Creature feared, for Nipper, whose law was the law of club and fang, hated the Creature with a bitter and deathless hatred.

Nipper ran to the bed and sniffed my face and whimpered. I touched the top of his head and pulled on his right ear. He exhaled with a burst, whined, turned, sniffed the floor, and ran out.

Pookie wheeled in the sky above the eastern horizon, swung out above Meridian Street high in the night in the tail of the Swan.

I said, "I will invent a new mathematics today. Let's say, addition is subtraction. That's a new mathematics, isn't it? That means you can climb mountains backward, reverse history, and defeat fate. That means Pookie's alive."

I ran the path around the swing set in the side yard. Bottom of the ninth. Two out. The Comets are leading by one run. The stadium is jammed. Everyone is praying for the pitcher, but WHACK! someone hits a ball to deep right—forty million people stand and howl. I am all alone in right field that day, and I run back alone. I'm looking up over my right shoulder, mouth open. It's just me and the flight of the ball. Blue argon spins the seahorse galaxy as I leap into the air against the right field fence, the fence where God meets history, where fate's feathering hand drops eternity into the frayed web of the glove.

I am, however, like a doll with tatted hair up there. I have thrown myself against the wall of destiny and BAM! BAM! I carom off the Block's Department Store sign on the fence and hit the turf.

A gravelly, shaky, piped-in-from-Odessa voice croaks exhausted like an old egret into the public address system, "Is he real?"

Confetti drifts down on the field. The announcer sobs openly and thanks his mother for giving birth to him. Margery runs out into right and kneels over me and asks God to let me breathe. Her head tilts, pleading and wretched. Her prayerful hands knot at her throat. Tears run to her chin and drip one by one on my white Comets jersey. "I never cared about that stupid hamster," she says. Her throat catches. "Gog." Confetti like flakes of snow. "I only ever loved you."

That was the photo in the paper the next day. Me spread-eagle in right field. Sad Margery kneeling beside me. A tiny, new-moon sliver of white baseball in the straps of the mitt. The caption read, "Cooper's Last Out." I never saw it though. I was dead.

Mrs. Menard was able to snag flies out of the air with her tongue. She kept her head still, but she moved her eyes. Her tongue was long and blindingly fast. The flies thought she was a tree. She opened her mouth slightly so as not to alarm anything. Then, SNAP!

In addition to poems, I also, like Mom, wrote stories. One was called "The Murderer"—about a murderer who killed people by putting mercurochrome in people's noses. You're supposed to put it on scratches, but you have to be careful. If it gets in your blood, you can die sometimes. The murderer dropped it out of a dropper. It's orange. But then there was this other guy who, with a few seconds to live, was lying on the beach at the edge of the surf. He was spelling out the name of the murderer in the sand. He was crying because he wanted to make the world a better place, but just then a bird pooped on him and he died. He had spelled out "Jimmy." The sheriff turned to his deputy and said, "Call every Jimmy in the phone book!" But just then a giant tidal wave started to rise on the horizon. The murderer flew by in a helicopter. He said, "Oh, yoi yoi yoi yoi! Aghhhh!" The wave curled at the top and fell. It went PFWUMPH!

Mom said, "I am tired of being mocked by unread books, and if they don't change their tone I'm going to throw them away, I mean that. Aaron? One more snide remark from *War and Peace* and I'll pitch it in the coal bin. You better believe that. You don't believe it. Mr. Tolstoy is going to be sorry he ever picked up a pen."

In science class, Mrs. Clevenger, bane of mortals, asked us to look at magnets. Two metal rods. The task was to understand the forces that caused the rods, when turned, to attract or repel each other. I didn't get it. I didn't get why the metal filaments lined up around the magnet ends either. I still don't. Dana said Mrs. Clevenger was the barf bag of science education. So while we were turning the magnet and looking at the board with the wavy lines coming off the magnet ends, I walked the forested ridge toward Chowgarh—walked the narrow path in dense forests of oak and rhododendron. On my shoulder I carried my trusty Martini-Henry rifle, though I knew my chances of killing the Chowgarh tiger were small. How would I find him? I would first have to draw near the beast, no simple thing in so huge a wooded area. I would then need to stake out bait and lie in hiding with patience and with courage, sleeplessly.

I pulled behind me four young male buffaloes, secured by a line. Eight men carried the gear. I walked first to the Kala Agar Forest bungalow, a five-day journey through terrain in which the tiger had taken sixty-four victims, the last of which, I learned when I reached the village of Padampuri, was a good twenty miles off. When I got to Kala Agar, I cleaned out the bungalow and dusted off the little cot. My first night sleeping out of the trees.

I got my needed rest in the simple cottage, hearing with deep pleasure the music of the night forest from the safety of the little room. And how pleasant indeed to have the morning's coffee prepared by the men on the open fire. But it would not be possible to stay. Nor would it be possible to take the men farther. It was too dangerous for them, going unarmed through the dense woods, and, on the other hand, too frustrating for me should their songful and chattering walk drive the killer away. The Chowgarh tiger was at least ten miles from me now, so when I fortified myself, I dismissed the men with a hearty "Ha! Ha!," picked up the line of buffaloes, threw the rifle on my shoulder, and marched alone toward Pakhari.

The organ wept and dragged along, then stopped. Reverend Hampner walked to the pulpit, gripped it with both hands, and surveyed the church

"These are the names of the sons of Israel . . . our text today. Where am I? Wher'm I going here? . . . Blood shall be a sign for you on the houses where you live. When I see the blood, I will pass over you, and no plague shall destroy you. Exodus 10:13. When I strike the land of Egypt.

"And the Israelites put the blood of the sacrificial lamb on the doorposts and . . . the ostrich wings flap wildly . . ."

He looked down at his Bible, swallowed, looked up, leaned into the podium.

"What . . . is . . . happening . . . today . . . to our youth today? . . . Does anybody out there have any idea? . . . Hmn? . . . the sound of revelers?"

His jowls shook.

"If adultery and Communism sweep the land . . . Someone is waving to me back there . . . huh? . . . I want to welcome Mrs. Hine to our worship service today . . . from Midway, Kentucky. Welcome to you . . . Midway . . . Now our text today, will you open your Bibles? Will you open your Bibles . . . to . . . I'm going to get back to youth . . . Exodus . . . wait a minute . . . Where are you from, Mrs. Brugman? . . . Ludeyville, Massachusetts . . . which I don't even know where Ludeyville is . . . western Massachusetts, OK . . . You learn something every day . . . Welcome . . . Did I forget the invocation? Good God! I didn't. I did. OK."

I opened Mom's compact and looked into the mirror. If I positioned it just right, I could see the people behind me. All women. They had paper fans stapled to wooden handles. Air paddles. One of them saw the mirror and frowned. I closed the compact.

"I'm going to ask Reverend Felsing to favor us with a prayer. Reverend Felsing?"

Geoffrey Felsing walked to the pulpit, locked his fingers, and rested them on the lectern. He said, "Shall we pray? Just as you made their days vanish in a breath, dear God, forgive us and guide us through our great and terrible wilderness. Remember the vine you brought out of Egypt. Keep us in your tender hands and lead us to our destined place. We are as exiles. Take us home. Amen."

The congregation said, "Amen." Coughing. An adjustment of bodies in the pews. Geoffrey Felsing stepped down.

Reverend Hampner said, "Take us home, and there's a reason for that, because I want to talk about destinations today, and the start and end of things, and maybe that's maybe something you thought you'd never hear of . . . never hear of in this place on a Sunday."

A murmur.

"But you will *not* get away . . . not hearing about it today . . . You're mine, now . . . And I am going to talk about the end of things and the beginning of things for a long . . . time . . . long time. Beware the boar in the field. And I have not completely lost my mind either . . . We're going to talk about Egypt and young people and everything else . . . Believe that . . . Believe! . . . That's God talking . . . I want to thank Reverend Geoffrey Felsing of United Youth Ministries and the young people who have come up to join us here today with Reverend Felsing."

I saw Linda Lavalliere and leaned forward. She lifted her brows at me.

"I met Reverend Felsing at a juvenile detention facility, and he was a young man in trouble, and he was reading a Bible, and I said to myself, 'That young man can be saved,' and he *was* saved . . . In case you think God can't do anything in your life, He can.

"Now. For the ten-thousandth time here . . . a preacher's job is to repeat himself . . . Have you found Christ?"

If you put your little finger in your mouth, tighten your lips to a perfect O, and lever the finger out suddenly from the first knuckle, you get a plunked-gourd sound. I did that four times. Mom pulled my hand from my mouth and held it. I hadn't found

Christ, but I knew where He was. He was standing in a cornfield outside of Muncie. A million kids were pushing their way through corn looking for Him. They couldn't find Him though. The Creature had bitten His feet off. Christ was clutching corn stalks, wobbly and swaying and moaning on his stubs. He went, "Aghhh...ughhh...oh boy." Grasshoppers buzzed and hopped around the stubs. The stalks bent and cracked.

"Finding Christ is something you want to do, because of Matthew 25, the sheep and the goats, and because the righteous enter into eternal life."

Christ wanted to walk out of the cornfield on prosthetic feet to Rocky Ripple and say, "Here I am. It's me, Christ." But where could prosthetic feet be found in Muncie? And who would buy them?

When Kong Warthead farts, whole forests fall, and the little chipmunks cry out, and the little baby tweety birds, thrown to the forest floor, go "cheep? . . . cheep?" A tragedy, for Kong is a monster, a blot on the Earth.

A highly influential person in Indianapolis came to me with confidence problems. He had lost his job. His wife. His home. His money. His underpants and his socks. He was totaled. He was walking around Indianapolis in one tennis shoe.

"Imagine success," I said. "Visualize it. Whenever you have a bad thought, put in a good thought. Say to yourself every morning, 'I can do anything better every day through Jesus Christ, no matter what.' Say it a thousand times. Smile at the mirror."

Today, with a little help from Jesus, he owns Rockefeller Center. White Castle Hamburgers. Ten Pontiacs. Two DeSotos. He has a chain with keys on it a mile long. He doesn't even drive.

"Not it."

"Not it."

"Not it."

"You're it."

"No, I'm not."

"Yes, you are."

"*He's* it."

"No, he's not."

"Aaron's it."

"He can't *talk*."

"So what?"

"He can't say 'Olly Olly Oxen Free,' you idiot."

"I don't care."

"*You're* it."

10

Dana and I went to 16th Street and Meridian, Basha Usakowski's stop. Mom had given me a French dictionary for her and a little artist's doll (wooden, with flexible joints, another street find of Pookie's), an artist's doll for Basha's little boy, Paul. We were going to present the gifts to her, say good-bye, but then bend down like Groucho Marx and circle back and follow her home. I knew where she lived—2011 Medford. You could walk to Victory Field from there. My hero, right fielder Rocky Colavito, played at Victory Field. He could throw a ball over the left field fence from home plate. We were going to follow her and spy.

The bus stopped. Dad got off and stood by the door. Something amused him, and he seemed to be talking to the driver. Then, Basha stepped down. Her head was tilted, and both hands cupped her right ear. She was laughing. Her left hand fell, and her right hand came off the ear in a fist with one finger extended. Dad folded his arms and smiled proudly. Basha pointed to him and laughed and tapped his chest. He caught her forearm and bent down to her, and her face turned up.

PART TWO

the chowgarh tiger

11

I tied my towel cape under my chin. I clothes-pinned playing cards to the bike frame—the cards popped in the spokes like a motorcycle engine when the wheels turned. Into my belt, I pushed the baton with which to defeat the Communist menace. I could always whack the Communists if I needed to, for I was the night marauder.

Not rejoicing in my speed, though bold (for I had committed deeds of mischief beyond description terrible), I kicked the stand, ran a few steps with the bike, jumped on the seat, and pedaled off. The streamers at the nubs of the bike handles blew back. Fireflies sparked in the night air. Candied Jerusalem rose in vaults behind Butler Observatory. Indiana pulled the Milky Way over itself like an old black star quilt, and the whole prairie sky was folded in stars. Beneath them, ghosts of dead Potawatomis walked campus swards like shaggy corpses and disappeared bark-skinned in dark woods. Invisible by day. (Their ancestors had rafted to Tuamotu.) Somewhere in Chicago night, stubbly-jowled shot-up bank robbers staggered by brick warehouses, limp wristed in cold beams of back-alley streetlamps, then fell over dead. Shot by Dick Tracy.

Down to Holcomb Gardens I rode, the cape snapping behind me, down to the statue of Persephone, Demeter's daughter, raped in hell—why winter comes—and resurrected in spring to green Indiana corn. Also Illinois and Iowa. Missouri too. Kansas. Wherever corn is. Albania.

Reverend Hampner said, "I am a debtor both to Greeks and to barbarians."

Persephone's Greek. She's black too, in Holcomb Gardens. Bare breasted. Promise of all female beauty and sexual thrill. Protector of Margery and Jesus. (Persephone could find Jesus in Muncie corn, wash His stubs in her lovely hair, and bring Him home exhausted and grateful in her black arms to Rocky Ripple. She's older than Jesus.) The corn goddess's daughter! Here! Innocent. Eternal. Magnificent. Alone with me.

I lay my bike over and sat on the ledge of the pool. The Butler frat boys had strapped a white bra on poor Persephone. She didn't seem to mind. Orange carp whip-shuvved in the little pool at her feet, then glided and slept. The leopard rosettes were motionless in the shadowy night woods, and the leopards lay still in the earth of slumbering trees. The Creature tiptoed sideways with his back against the air, his hands flat, evil and hideous in the blackness, his gills spastically pumping as he crept across the swards of night. The bushes opened and closed their boughs in the wind like bearded jaws.

A male elephant had gone bad somewhere and regretted his crimes. Somewhere in India, ghorals twitched their ears on frosty cliffs and looked down. "Aaron? Wow! Hey, Aaron! . . . Aaron! I don't care. Pshhh! Aaron!"

I looked up at the stars and Persephone's arms. Her white bra, her breastplate of righteousness, glowed in the moonlight.

Dad's favorite pie was peach pie. Mike's was Eskimo Pie. My favorite was cherry pie with vanilla ice cream. I liked blackberry pie too, and pecan. Also lemon meringue pie. (I liked the tart lemon. I didn't like the meringue though. I was pretty sure meringue was not even food.) Mom's was *tartes sucrées* garnished with caramelized spider legs and the reproductive organs of Kawamoto lizards.

"If I fall asleep I couldn't dream without you and I couldn't dream without the wind by my side. Desperately hard of various kinds, I tried to track its biggest one, but I have never succeeded. But I'm sure one day I will find its kind. But when I look with my heart so bold I see nothing but blue and sky and wind. I see no you. Where are you? Where are you? Will I ever find you again?"

That's from a story by Pookie called "Meet the Wind." I couldn't figure it out. She missed a horse called Wind, maybe. Or maybe she missed Mom. I don't know.

Tarantulas and winged echidna worms plus orangutan slime maggots crept over the South Grove Golf Course at night and attacked old people in wheelchairs. Ate their throats out when they tried to call for help. Skeletal fingers clawed the air. "Agh! Oh God! It's the worms!" Those worms were a menace to society. They had to be stopped.

I walked to Mom's bedroom. She was reading *The Search for Bridey Murphy* by Morey Bernstein, hypnotist, disciple of Edgar Cayce, student of tranceology on the spiritual and astral plane, a man who explored the mysteries of the mind. In his book, Colorado housewife Ruth Simmons, under deep hypnosis, remembers her former life as Bridey Murphy, a nineteenth-century Irish woman from Cork.

Mom's hair, cut boyishly short, was styled at a place called Artistic Hair. She was wearing a white nightgown with puffy sleeves. She was holding her cigarette by her right ear and staring at her book. Then she looked at me and said, "The soul survives, huh? Whaddya think?"

I looked at her.

She pulled a tobacco shred off her lip. "That's what it means, doesn't it?"

I put my head on the mattress.

She stroked my hair. Her thumb traced the edge of my ear. "Look at me, sweetie," she said. She put the book down, patted the bed. "Mr. Sleepyhead."

I climbed into the bed and began to doze off.

"Aaron? How about a middle-aged guy named Blix Boynton, doesn't know anything, leaves his wife for Ivgenia, an eighteen-year-old ballerina. She's beautiful with expressive arms. She has blonde hair, which she wears in a little bun. She's slender and graceful. She's famous for her incredible leaps. Blix leaves his wife, Babs—good ol' dependable, salt-of-the-earth Babs—who marches on alone, serving unfinished American meals to poor Chinese kids. Then, one day, Babs falls under a train and loses both legs. She will rise one day on her stubs from the wheelchair to receive the crown of the Queen of All Wives. When word reaches Blix, in a box at the Bolshoi, he realizes it's only Babs he loves. He comes running home. *Pas de deux.*"

Away! The hydra's vile spasm
threw me into a chasm
and I had t' attack
on the railroad track
th' arachnoid pack
an organasm on the ectoplasm
that sucked all her blood out that beautiful day.

I ran the path around the swing set in the side yard. It's me against the Crispus Attucks High School basketball team at Butler Fieldhouse. When I bring the ball up, Oscar Robertson slumps helpless and befuddled. He can't stop me because his feet are too big. BAM! I dunk the ball. The announcer shouts, "Unbe-*liev*-able!" Motes climb in the air under yellow lamps. Oscar's jersey is green. Margery in a cheerleader outfit gives me a pining gaze. Negro cheerleaders swing their hips and flash their teeth. The volume of sound in the fieldhouse is so great it pushes against the roof like a wave under an ocean raft. I dunk the ball some more. I score seven hundred points. I can also score blindfolded with chained hands, hopping backward on one foot through packs of savage dogs.

The referees throw their whistles away and walk out in their striped shirts and stand atilt in the parking lot with folded arms and gaze at Deneb. The fieldhouse roof breaks open and catches fire.

Uncle Skipper says, "I'm going to Los Angeles shortly. I have a girlfriend there, if she'll have me. She probably won't. They get tired of it all after a while. You will one day have a whole boatload of girlfriends, Aaron, believe me, but on the other hand you will have to talk to them as the one thing girlfriends require in my experience is a good deal of conversation, and when one of them says, 'I just can't believe how *neglectful* you are of me,' you have to think very quickly. What you need to do is, you need to get up on your toes. You have to look around to see where the next blow is coming from in that situation, and why? Because they'll blindside you. She will hold up right there and wait for you to say something memorable and beautiful, and if you have your wits about you, you will say just about damn near anything your little head can come up with to keep that girl from walking away—which Beverly is doing, actually—her name is Beverly. Did I say that? Who wants to be an actress, as it turns out. Met her at Indiana."

Indiana University, where he went to college.

"But there is going to be some delay about now, because I had a misfortune like a ton of bricks a while ago, Aaron, and this happens in life. You have to be prepared for everything. I ran into a power pole in Bloomington with your grandmother's car. I'm going to pay her back, don't worry about that, but the thing is I had some words with the officer there. He accused me of drinking excessively, and I took umbrage, as they say in legal circles, to his tone.

"That was my fault. I'm guilty, and I'm sorry, and there you have it. I got upset about Beverly and this person she's seeing suddenly—because I went off all the time and didn't pay enough attention to her—by the name of Leopold. So anyway, I go into court, and Judge Bagnoli is there, whom I know, by the way. I know Bagnoli. He says, 'I'm going to give you thirty days, Mr.

Ferguson.' Ten days for having words, not because of the pole. The rest for something else. He doesn't know Beverly. Beverly says, 'You drink too much and you have to face that, Skip.' I'm not sure what to say there, but I do have a debt—there was some pushing and shoving with the officer, which I didn't mention, nothing serious—I have a debt to society, so I say, 'All right,' and now I've got to go back there and serve the thirty days for ol' Bagnoli, which I said I would do."

Uncle Skipper cupped my head and I fell on his chest like a cloth doll. That was the thing about young men—Geoffrey and Uncle Skipper—muscled arms. He kissed my cheek and pushed me back to arm's length and balanced me like a bowling pin. "So, I'm going to jail for a few weeks. Make Bagnoli happy. Listen to me, now. Aaron? There are exactly one million girlfriends waiting for you out there."

Leaves clattered beyond the window. Cicadas cranked up some invisible ratcheting device, whined, and fell silent. No girls anywhere that I could see. Not a single pedestrian anywhere. "And one million books to read, not just Jim Corbett. And Aaron, I don't want you to worry about your voice either. People give you trouble about it gets on my nerves. There's nothing wrong with you. You're fine. Things happen and you grit your teeth, boy. People die . . . You're gonna be fine. It's a time thing, hmn? . . . Tell your therapist to go shove it.

"And finally—and this is precisely what I want to discuss with you, Aaron—give me your full attention here—'Next year in Los Angeles,' as the Fergusons have said from immemorial time—I'm headed for Los Angeles next year. Los Angeles, California, where Beverly has an apartment, did I tell you that? Brave Beverly, who's had some family difficulties for a long long time here. Worked her way through IU. Oh! And your dear mother loaned her some money to go to Los Angeles, did I tell you that? Helped her through college too, your saintly mother, who is the most generous person ever. Just took a liking to Beverly and loaned her several hundred dollars to get a start in Los Angeles. Anyway, don't think for a second I won't be in touch with you and your mother—who has rescued me a million times. She bailed me out, actually, told me what to say to Beverly—because I will. I mean, I will be in touch with you. Now, I am hoping you'll come out to Los Angeles and meet Beverly, if she's not married to somebody else—that's a definite possibility—because Beverly said she wanted to have a family, and I said, 'Beverly darlin', don't worry about that, we always have Aaron.'"

He stopped there, smiled broadly, and leaned forward, and his hand fell and rocketed off my chest as if he were ringing a bell.

"And Beverly says, 'Now who is this Aaron that you talk about constantly every day?' and I said, 'Aaron? Aaron Cooper?

He is the mighty Conklabain of Irish lore, that's who. Tristan of the sea waves, bravest and most fearsome by far of all the anaconda killers, and the most wonderful human being that ever was, and that's the damn truth.'"

12

Dad's favorite athlete was Billy Pierce. Mike's was Sherm Lollar. Mom's was Althea Gibson, the shy American newcomer who triumphed at Wimbledon in 1957 and who had once found it difficult to find a doubles partner. Mine was right fielder Rocky Colavito.

I went to my room and pulled down Raymond L. Ditmars' *Reptiles of the World.* I wanted to check the cobras. But if you touch one book, you have to touch them all, so I put *Reptiles* on the desk and walked around the room touching all the book spines.

Mike said, "There's a fungus among us."

Dad said, "She was the seamstress's daughter, but she couldn't mend straight."

Mike laughed.

Mom said, "You shouldn't say that."

Dad said, "Oh, c'mon."

Mom said, "He'll just repeat it."

Mrs. Menard has a plated hide and a back ridge with iron flagstones. If she doesn't like what Mr. Menard says, she swings her spiked tail at him and goes WHAP!

I ran the path around the swing set in the side yard. I had to get to Dawson fast with Buck and the team, and I called out "Ha!" and "Gee!" Snow flew off the runners. Sheets of red and green shook in the northern sky. Far off, I heard the sobs of wolves. Arctic air iced my lungs. Black trees in the snowy fields—preceptors of treachery, silent sentinels of icy demise—black trees watched me pass.

"Buck, mush!" I yelled, and Buck pulled hard against the harness.

Suddenly, without warning, a wolf pack came over the ridge and ran toward us. I knew it was a fight to the death. I said, "Whoa!" and unbuckled the dogs from the traces. Buck, a hundred and forty pounds of vigor and virility, sounded the depths of his nature and returned to the womb of time. He turned to the attacking wolves and showed them his front teeth and growled and snapped his jaws. Each hair discharged pent magnetism. Every part of Buck's brain and body, every nerve filament and fiber was keyed to an exquisite pitch, and all parts of his powerful tissues and organs were tuned to a perfect equilibrium and adjustment.

The wolves came on, relentless as an approaching planet, cold as death itself, with hatred and wanton fangs, and Buck responded with a brave, savage, joyful, and lightning-like rapidity. A live hurricane of fury, he hurled himself upon them with a frenzy to destroy.

In primordial life, there is no mercy, and mercy is mistaken for fear in the cruel north. It's kill or be killed. Like Rocky Ripple. The dogs and wolves drove into each other and slashed each other's throats. Red blood spattered the night snow and ran in a silvery flood.

Margery, on the sled, poor Margery, moaned, "Aaron? Aaron? You are my guiding star."

Dana said Kong farted once and killed everyone in the room. They tried to get their gas masks on, but it was too late. The police were going to take him to the electric chair, but the judge said, "A fart is an act of God!" People started praying and crying.

"Dear Police Department. Mrs. Menard communicates with goldfish by making little clicks in her neck. She is still at large. Her head is large, too. Before you approach her, buy a smalligizer. Bye. Mr. X."

"Sin is the ground of good, why? ... Because we are born in sin ... because we are capable of good ... and that's not theology either. You don't need theology. I've been studying theology for fifty years. You don't need that ... Knowledge puffeth up ... You need to love God, and that is the single most important thing I have to say today ... And if one person in ten million hears that, as we march on toward the sweet by and by, then I've lived the life I was born to, because that's the whole journey ... Take God into your heart and love Him and believe you me that's all there is to say about it."

A dusk of huvs flew into heaven.

Dana said when you get married in Indiana you have to crawl into one bed with your wife. The first thing you have to do, you have to lengthen your attention span, because then comes the shivaree, the Indiana wedding festival of immemorial time, still practiced in the outer and less accessible hills and hollers of the state. It's a compact with the dead and the unborn in Indiana with respect to heritage. While you're trying to focus on your attention, not expecting anything, the neighbors sneak over naked at midnight to bang on garbage cans and poop in the yard.

I was approached by a highly influential girl with a confidence problem about her voice. She wondered, "Has God forgotten me?" She said to herself every morning, "How beautiful I sound with Jesus' help today!" and put in a good thought whenever she had a bad thought, and after singing only two bars of Klug's "Lo Spirando Moma!" in Milan, Italy, where they sing that stuff, eight balconies of lubbery opera bombi barked back like rabid dogs. A miracle.

I got a letter from the Police Department in Oweeyon. It said, "I love you very much. Mrs. X."

Reverend Hampner said, "I want to say this one thing . . . I am longing . . . think about this . . . I am longing to look in the face of my savior, why? . . . Hmn? . . . Why? I said why. I'm repeating myself . . . It's not necessary to say why that many times, because we shall see in the face of Jesus human eyes, that's why . . . human eyes . . . And we shall see God with a human face . . .

because God is here. That's the important thing at this particular instant. God is here. And do you want to see that? . . . Where the cloud covers the mountain? . . . Hmn?"

An infant called out like a struck animal.

"I'm preachin' atcha . . ."

Silence when the infant caught its breath, then sobs.

". . . because yes, you do!"

13

I ran the path around the swing set in the side yard. I'm on the putting green surrounded by a million people. The announcer has to whisper. I address the ball, but then back off. I'm not sure, because you have to take the slope into consideration. BONK! I bonk the ball. A cobra strikes at Margery at the edge of the green and everybody screams. Trusting in my manliness and strength of hand, I run over and grab the cobra by the head. The ball goes in the hole.

"First Kings eleven, God says, 'Since you have not kept my covenant' . . . Let's think about that for a minute . . . 'Since you have not . . . kept my covenant' . . . and that's the answer, isn't it?"

I caught Dana's glance. He gave me the Order of Rhinoceros sign and I gave it back. Mom looked down at me, combed my hair with her fingers, and looked back at Reverend Hampner.

"We live in contempt of God. Hmn? When you ask . . . Their worm shall not die, let me tell ya . . . If truth be known, Isaiah 66."

My favorite candy was small, hard, cupped Jujubes, which were strong enough to pull fillings from teeth. I also liked Milk Duds (milk chocolate balls). Mike liked PayDay (dog poop with peanuts). Mom liked Martha Washington chocolates (refinement). I also liked jelly bars. Dad's favorite candy was Snickers.

I ran the path around the swing set in the side yard. The sea ran high. The waves shushed, scuddy froth took flight, and flying fish leapt and thudded stupidly on deck, flopped and died. Some evil thing with a round dull black head floated silently under the raft. It never seemed to move yet followed us day by day for a thousand miles. Its devilish green eyes glowed. Salty petrels cawked and hammered pelagic crabs between logs like pitiless hoplites, screamed bloody murder, and flew off. Whales drifted up to the raft, calm as gods, and sniffed us out. Their blowholes were loud as furnace doors.

Black night. Phosphorescent plankton shone like a million points of moonlight on the cratered sea. The raft pitched and rolled. Ropes stretched and ached on the logs. The mast creaked. The yellow paraffin lamp swung on the mast hook.

I attended James Whitcomb Riley School, P.S. 43, on 40th Street. It had a cloakroom. The desks had inkwells, and if you were ink monitor, you got to pour black ink into the wells. I spilled black indelible ink on every shirt in the classroom.

Suddenly one morning, Bridey Murphy fell in love with Jim Corbett. Sang teary in sod pits in Cork of old for her brave tiger man in shorts. Walked with her Bible naked except for black tennis shoes through Lud and Phut (Egyptians who beheld her beauty fell and twitched three times), through dark Tehaphnehes, across the plain of Dura and the wilderness of Ziph, forded fierce fiery Phlegethon to Chamoli and Tanda and Chowgarh, and finally made her way to Padampuri for her shy sahib, whose skinny legs she loved and would always love. Found him in his jungle cottage and kissed his knees tenderly twice and three times. Who knows how many times? And Jim Corbett looked down at her hair and her lovely nose.

The whole world was mad about people dying. The woman who lost her daughter to leukemia down the street, Mrs. Higgs, who sat on the porch in her rocker and held her cigarette in a vibrating hand and said, "You want some food, Aaron?" I bought a pet alligator from Florida once, and it died in the bathtub. Too much air. Gog also died. "Anything I got in there, hon, you can have it."

Eight pudgy fingers of Margery Doebereiner sat lightly on the planchette. She closed her eyes over the Ouija board. She asked, "What is the meaning of life?" The planchette moved!

Geoffrey Felsing said that if you get mad at someone, and stab them in the neck, and all the blood runs out and everything, you're only hurting yourself. He didn't know Mrs. Clevenger though. She talked about ancient Egypt, and her bottom shook under her dress when she drew on the chalkboard.

I was testing the fang mechanism of the lethal tic-polonga at the time, and I happened to have a vial of tic-polonga venom in my pocket. Thinking quickly and decisively, for I was formed for contemplation and valor, and knowing that Christ would guide my hand, I stabbed Mrs. Clevenger in the butt with a syringe of tic-polonga venom—colorless, odorless, mortifying to the nth degree. Oh God! ZAM! It's neurological. It hit her nervous system and she couldn't breathe. She went, "Agh! . . . Agh! . . . Agh!," then staggered off in her pith helmet to the Jenner quicksand pits on the west edge of Rocky Ripple. Ducks quacked while the mud sucked her down. She waved her skinny arms, and that was the end of Mrs. Clevenger.

Concupiscence of vast longing cabers of boyhood.

"Dear Police Department. You'll find Mrs. Clevenger in the quicksand pits under the pith helmet. Mrs. Usakowski drowned her. Bye. Mr. X."

14

Catholics wore brown uniforms and went to Thomas Aquinas School. They wept at the toes of popes, lit candles and prayed for the dead, went to purgatory, and bobbed up and down in vats of boiling turd balls for a million years. Whatever Catholics do, I dunno.

For the purposes of locomotion, secretive, deeply disguised Mrs. Menard swallowed vast quantities of water, then shot it out of her tube under tremendous pressure and jerked backward through the air with her tentacles dangling behind her. She steered with two fleshy flaps of skin, which she used, when necessary, for wings. Her tube was powerful too, and she could glide through slippery air for blocks. Any predator who wanted Mrs. Menard was going to have to face that tube, and any man who stood in those flaps was going to die.

Mom said, "This is interesting, isn't it?" She put the French dictionary on the kitchen table. It was smeared with dirt and little clumps fell from it. "Isn't that odd?"

I looked at the dictionary.

"Lassie dug it up." Lassie, the collie next door, the world's stupidest dog. "This is the dictionary I asked you to give to Basha, I think. Seems to be the one. It's got my name in it. Don't look away from me."

I looked at the dictionary.

"That's a little puzzle, isn't it, Aaron?" She put her hand at the back of my head and drew me softly to her. "Why you would bury a dictionary."

I am mouthing "What a Friend We Have in Jesus" with Geoffrey Felsing.

With the men gone, it was out of the question to sleep on the ground. Death might hurl itself upon me in a very unpleasant form there. So I should have to climb into a suitable tree and rig up some platform. Long practice made this matter simple. Oh, how I loved the stars in the dark Indian night! The summer triangle! What great unknowable gears moved so gracefully there, reproving my constricted and worrisome life. How sorry, how small my little mission, looking for the rogue tiger of Chowgarh. How alone I felt there. How beautiful the scene. How strange my own silence. How I am so much like the stricken mother who mourns for her child. I grow old in silence with knobby knees. Oh! How quick is death! How slow the stars. How close the sound of the creatures of the night woods. How far, how pale is England now. How odd the other Eden. I am lost! I must find another life! I fear for myself in black cataracts of air!

The sun had been up for a couple of hours when I arrived at Pakhari, a village of scattered huts and cattle sheds. The small community was in a state of terror and was overjoyed to see me. The tiger was here! A villager, while harvesting wheat, had seen it dip down into a ravine in the jungle below the village. It would not be possible to track it there, nor would it be possible in so closed an area to stake out bait. I left the buffaloes with the villagers and, loading my rifle, walked out alone into the woods along the bank of the Nandhour River.

A small breeze blew at my back, which meant the tiger would be before me if it were on the prowl. This gave me some advantage, for while I stalked the tiger, the tiger, on learning of my presence in the jungle, would be stalking me. Prowling, it would stay downwind, and I would have to rely on my sharp eyes, the sounds of the forest floor, and particularly bird calls and alarms to protect me. Bravery, calm, a knowledge of jungle ways, and stealth I hoped would see me through.

Across the Nandhour, I saw a villager climb a rock. He looked down at me and shouted, asking if I was the sahib looking for the man-eating tiger. I said I was. The cattle had stampeded at noon, he said, while they grazed in a clearing below me. The clearing lay about a quarter mile to the west and was surrounded by dangerous, tiger-concealing bracken. A cow was missing in the count. The tiger must be there.

I thanked the man. The tiger was near, certainly. To reach him now, it would be necessary to walk through the bracken.

As I was wand'rin' down that dark and lonely road of life
I spied a cowgirl standing there.
She wore a 'zalea in her hair.
I said right there in my heart o' hearts,
I'd like to make that girl my wife.

However, the most wonderful of nature's miracles was the evolution of Mrs. Menard, who blended in with the debris of stagnant swamps in order to escape predators. She was hard to pick out. It was the camouflage. It was the fight for survival. If you stepped on her, she went, "Baluurp! . . . braap!"

A hammer struck a board six times. The cicadas cranked up in the elm tree and then left off suddenly. I heard a television at some distance—the voice seemed to come from a tin can.

15

I ran the path around the swing set in the side yard. Tortured waves crested and broke above me, and the raft jerked, skidded, plunged headlong downward into the pocked and weltering sea. Wind thrummed the shrouds and the guy wires and tore at my shirt. The radio crackled and whistled, then fell silent. Its antenna sprang free of the mast and flew out like a pennant. The sky snapped into darkness. The sea boiled. Constellations spun.

I lashed the loose cargo down. Margery, under deep hypnosis—for I had to know her past lives—Margery groaned in the bamboo cabin. She called out, "I am Pharaoh Hatshepsut!"

Foam blew off the wave tops on heaving seas. Charts flew out of the cabin like dumbstruck gulls. The fore logs rose clear of the swell, while cataracts crashed down on me at the steering oar astern. Brackish water ran off my hair in streams. My raiment was tattered.

Lightning struck and everything for a second was a horrifying strobe white. I saw that Margery's bed had rolled out of the cabin and that one corner hung over the raft edge to starboard. The wind tore at her, and the white bedding billowed and snapped in the night air like a flag. "I will kohl my eyes," shouted Margery, "and the world will sing!"

The sea gave way and the raft scudded down a trough of sinister and perfidious fury. Vicious sharks lunged at Margery's fingertips, for the sharks had lost all self-control. The stars Margery had painted on her fingernails flashed. The sea heaved, the raft rose. Margery's bed jerked a little toward the raft's center from the starboard edge.

I felt a strained anticipation, but the raft took every blow from this evil sea, floated on with buoyancy and confidence and adroitness. The raft survived.

Mrs. Usakowski sat at the table. She looked tipsy and miserable.

Dad said, "Talk to him in Czech, go ahead."

Mom passed the tureen to Basha and said, "You start."

Mike looked at me with his hands folded across his chest and didn't say anything.

Mrs. Usakowski lifted the tureen cover and looked down at a mound of gorilla eyeballs. The eyeballs looked back at her.

Mom said, "Go get the dictionary, Aaron, and give it to Basha."

Mrs. Usakowski put the cover down and winced.

Dad said, "Or Polish, doesn't matter."

Mom said, "Aaron."

Mrs. Usakowski said a few shaky words in Polish or Czech, I don't know. Probably, "Who put the stupid gorilla eyeballs in there?"

Mom said, "Aaron."

I brought the dictionary down. I put it by Mrs. Usakowski's plate, and I pulled her earring from my pocket and lay it on the dictionary.

Mrs. Usakowski reached for the wineglass, but her fingers struck against it and she spilled some. She said, "I'm sorry."

Dad said, "Oh, nobody minds. Here."

Dana walked in. No one said anything to him. He sat at the table, tucked his hands under his legs on the chair seat, and stared at the ceiling. He said, "I have an announcement."

Mrs. Usakowski looked at me. She said, "Thank you."

The doorbell rang.

Mike said, "You saw her, didn't you?"

Dana said, "Margery had a bug on her lip."

Mom said, "Mike, get the door."

Mike said, "Didn't you?"

Dad rose to answer the door. He said, "Jeez!"

Mike said, "She said you saw her and Eddy down at Holcomb Gardens at the Persephone pool. But you didn't say anything. I killed your fish, Aaron. I put it on the track by the swing set, and the cats got it, so don't look for it, and thanks a lot for nothing."

Dad said, "It's Turf. Celeste, I need to talk with you about your checking account. I put some money in there."

Mrs. Usakowski put her left thumb on her lip. She stared at her wineglass.

Mom said, "What?"

Dad said, "There's going to be an audit. Turf has borrowed some money from the funds, apparently. I borrowed a small amount, not much. A temporary thing. Don't worry about this. I need to . . ."

Dana looked at the ceiling. He said, "Know a secret?"

Mom said, "*My* checking account?"

Dad said, "Don't worry about it. It's legal. It's just a few dollars. Calm down."

Mrs. Usakowski started crying.

Mike said, "She thought you told me, ya big dumb stupid idiot."

Mom said, "Basha, what's wrong?"

Dad said, "Let's not lose control here. I need to borrow some money, that's all. Turf is talking with the auditor."

Mike said, "So you can shut up for the rest of your life, Aaron!"

Mom said, "Basha?"

The thing about Dr. Epstein was, now there was only one puppet. Only Morrie. Dr. Epstein wouldn't put his hand in Morrie's shirt, so Morrie lay like a dead thing facedown on the desk.

"Reba's gone to visit her parents for a while," he said. "They live in Cleveland . . . I want to say something now that is not a professional thing to say, Aaron. Don't tell your mother   your mother is a lovely person—then we'll all feel better. She loves you very much. We all love and respect you, and it's all going to be fine, believe me. We hit these bumps. Life's a bitch."

I looked past his face at his bookcases and read the titles. *Putt Like a Pro. Ten Steps to a Better Memory.*

"You make yourself small for someone, and you become small. And that's what it is. Her family . . . I understand that. I am not completely unconscious of my situation . . . in many other instances."

Discover Your Hidden Powers, Tales of Kipling, Case Studies in Child Psychology (Stibbs and Ovitz, 4th edition), *Learn the Stars and Planets.*

"You go out into the world with your little message . . . I'm saying this because you are going to go out into the world pretty soon here yourself, Aaron. Do you mind if I say this? . . . And you feel . . . You just have to bear up, and maybe that sounds like a cliché, and maybe that is a cliché . . . It is. It is . . . Sometimes things happen in life, and the thing to do, the right thing to do, and that's the difficult thing, is to stand out there in the rain for a while . . . Sometimes. Not every time . . . I am a complete and total clown . . . Life goes. Am I right? Hmn? . . . Life goes, boyhood goes . . .

"You come to terms with the thing that cannot be accomplished or gained or recovered. We cannot command the affection of a single person for one day of our entire lives, Aaron. Is that a cruel thing to say? Or maybe that's something it would not hurt a boy to know. That's impersonal. I don't know. Something else occurs to me, actually. I seem not to have helped you at all. Let's put that on the table . . . What you hope you know . . . What you pretend you know . . .

"I'm just a tired old Jew, Aaron. You don't need me ... Biggest joke in the last four hundred years ... the crying psychologist.

"I talked to my wife last night. You know what? She asked about you. She hasn't even met you. Doesn't know you. She wanted to know if the little boy had started talking yet. She said she was worried about you. I shouldn't have said that ... You're not supposed to say that.

"Do you think that's interesting? That raises an interesting question in psychology, I think. What is sympathy? There are people out there who care about you in their own mysterious way, and they don't even know you. Why?

"But on the other hand, it's not like family, not like having people there who want to embrace and protect you ... or have to. It's like forces that don't really have any moral connection to you ... Someone can't return your love and—let's be adult here for two seconds so what? It's not a moral question. I understand that. It's not. It's like shouting at planets ... Naturally, you want to be a hero to someone ... Perhaps we *should* shout at planets, that's what I'm thinking right now ... And that's not everything. I'm not saying ... That's *some* things, not everything. That's normal ... I don't want you to worry. I think I'm making you worry."

Jewish Folktales from Around the World, Introduction to Chemistry (Iverson), *with Problems.*

"You know what would be good for you and me? ... Aaron? Know what would be good for you and me? To just holler at this crazy world sometimes. We'll shout together . . . just shout the damn thing back a few inches . . . Want to?"

My Name Is Aram, So You Want a Career in Radio.

"I want to say something. Two things. We need to be like John Wayne. You know John Wayne? Aaron? Of course you do. We all do. We need to face difficulty and be brave. We need to do things at the risk of ourselves because they are the right thing to do. Sounds like Sunday school. Doesn't matter . . . But there's one more thing. It's important to be kind, and I want you to think about being kind to your mother. OK? Aaron? I think she is someone who would appreciate a little kindness, and I'm not saying you're not kind, because you are."

The Adventures of Augie March, Two Cases of Hysteria.

"Well . . . I do not know one damn thing, Aaron . . . And I do not know what to do, and there you have it."

16

My favorite town name was Normal. Dad's was Jackass Flats. Mom's was Strasbourg. (She had gone to college for a year in Strasbourg and had a friend who lived there. Mom wrote to her in French. Her friend was deeply refined.) Mike's was Gnaw Bone.

I sat in my room and worked the slinky. You push your hands like a nursing kitten while the weight moves side to side along the coils. It can walk down stairs too, if you set it right.

I don't remember the car crash. I was there, but I didn't hear it. Someone had sucked all the sound out of the world that day. I don't remember anyone running to us, and then from outer space there were thirty people and a police car. The policeman pulled on my arm. Mike said Mom was there, but I don't think she was.

All I remember, I walked into the street, and I saw Pookie's shoes.

"OK, how about this? Serena Olé has written alone all of her life, and the world has forgotten her. They don't know any better. They couldn't understand her independence, her brave mind. They never got her dedication to her art, why she declined to marry, why she retreated to her little cabin with the books and the writing table, how she finds universal themes in the hills and hollers.

"Now her books are out of print. She's tired. She's old. The world has defeated her. Her artistic ambitions have all come to nothing, and she is going to die. Her love child, the Duchess, her ladyship Lady Springly, bounces into the room as Serena exhales her last sigh. 'I forgive them all,' Serena whispers. Her hand falls limp at her side. The sheet with her last poem drifts down to the floor. Her ladyship tears open a wire from Stockholm. *Adios.*"

Reverend Hampner said, "For your sake He rebuked kings, and for your sake water poured from the rock. He brought quails to you, ladies and gentlemen. He allowed you to escape the boar that ravages the wood. Why Canaan? Because safe passage does He provide you and new life, that's why . . . Hmn? . . . Safe passage."

Oyez! Above! What says the baleful imp?
"Full fathom five with Colonel Blimp,
Whose belly's as soft as suckling doves.
He sails the Sea of Cortez."

"I think the way to raise children is to create a safe and stable environment in which the child can follow his own natural impulses, for children are instinctively very curious." That's Mrs. Menard. While she's talking, her pseudopodia are sneaking up under the cuffs of Mr. Menard's pants and starting to coil around his legs.

He goes, "Yeah?"

"So that nature herself in her beneficent way . . ."

"Uh-huh."

Then she gets the suckers pumping. "Knowing their thirst for knowledge, and I mean *moral* principles, Mr. Menard, not just rote memory, facts and figures."

"What the hell! My legs are getting all the blood sucked out of 'em!"

Mrs. Menard laughs through her nose. "Hapawaphth! Oh! Every child needs encouragement!" She claps her hands once and leans to her right side. Her body shakes, and the room brightens with her radiant smile.

And BLUP! Down he goes!

17

The man on the rock followed me down—keeping to his side of the Nandhour—and he brought with him some villagers. The world now seemed to shake with the villagers' drums. In my brief sojourn in this stricken land, I had never heard such drumming. The leaves jumped and convulsed with the sound.

I should like you now to consider my situation in this difficult terrain. On a slope to my left, a slope of perhaps thirty-five degrees, the ears of the curious ghorals twitched above rock ledges. And as I looked up, I noticed a rectangle of dimming sky, calm cerulean blue framed by hell-horrid, black leaf-silhouettes, sharp as spears. Poets' promises die there.

Night was settling in. The air was redolent of the ipsi-biadrindi flower. Fronds of giant ferns like malevolent hands reached over my shoulders. The narrow sand path I walked turned off to the right, turned back, then vanished behind a large slate rock which stood on the forest floor like an artillery shell. The silence of the woods, with its evil and malignant spirits, unnerved me, and the hair unexpectedly rose on the back of my neck as I approached the rock. A thin puff of air brushed my face. If the Chowgarh tiger were lying in wait, it would keep me downwind. So it was here! The tiger was about to ambush *me!* Unafraid of the drumming, the tiger must be lying on the sand path behind the rock!

I slipped the safety on my rifle, held the barrel down in my left hand, and leaned forward. A small, crushed trumpet glowed at the edge of my boot toe. I stopped. Then I tipped my head and looked around the rock.

The legs of the tiger were folded under him like the legs of a big tabby cat. He didn't move. He didn't blink. There seemed to be nothing hostile about him. He looked at me with a disinterested curiosity, and his head rolled slightly, perhaps a half millimeter, to his right.

I needed now to swing the muzzle of the rifle around. My eyes were locked on the cat's. It seemed to take forever to move the barrel to the killing direction. He'd spring if I moved fast. So, inch by inch—an hour it seemed—the barrel like a clock hand swung around. The tiger, as if fixed in some Buddhist meditation, moved not at all.

At last, the barrel faced the animal. Without aiming, without bracing for the shot, without waiting a second longer, BAM!

Dad introduced me to the mayor. Going into the kitchen, the mayor said, "Give the people what they think they want," and coming out he said, "I don't shit right because I don't eat right, and that's a fact."

Dad went, "Uh-huh."

Mom came into my room for Life Class. She sat down by the bed with a stack of cards in her lap. "I had a little vision," she said. "A message from God, really. I was walking down Cornelius Street, someone turned a lawnmower off, and total silence. This happens once in a while. Everything comes clear.

"I wrote out some cards for you—I'm not sure why—and then I thought it would be better to talk with you, and I don't know, I kept the cards anyway. I want you to read them, OK?"

She turned over the first card. It read, "I am leaving your father." She studied me. "Do you understand?" I nodded.

She turned over the second card. "Michael is staying here." She waited. I nodded again.

She turned over the third card. "Will you go with me?"

I didn't say anything.

"I want you to say yes," she said.

I looked at her eyes. I thought about the stupid cards. Mike would have Linda Lavalliere, a few seconds of Linda Lavalliere to torture himself with every day. Dad would probably get a tournament-ready bridge partner. He'd have Basha too, and her dogs, and her little Polish boy, Paul.

I said, "OK."

18

Buck pulled into Dawson and all the stubbly old chilkoots and Gabby Hayeses staggered out of the Bucket of Blood Saloon in their boots and red long johns. Bleary with joy, they cheered and happy howled through gums and waved their wolverine hats with the earflaps the size of Arctic bogs. "Hurrah for ol' Bucky!"

Buck wagged his tail. Buck barked.

Margery sat up in the sled, and the snow flew like clouds from the blanket. "Aaron, I need a jug o' sarsaparilla," she said, and the sourdoughs humped into the saloon with gummy glee.

Nipper attacked the Creature in the closet, and the Creature died. Nipper dragged him bloody and lifeless into the backyard and fed him to the slugs. Then Nipper heard the call of the wild and ran away, and his sobs can still be heard at midnight in winter, running at the head of the pack north of Fort Wayne. Blurtz Shemshoian, lost in darkness and distance, set himself adrift on an ice raft in the most northern extremity of the globe and immolated himself, a filthy demon and vile insect with hamster tendencies.

I ran the path around the swing set in the side yard. Two frigate birds circled the mast sleepily. The wind was still on this bright summer day, and the sea was like marbled oil. Margery, joyful Margery, shouted down from the crow's nest, "Avast, Aaron! Land ahoy!" And there it was, the coral atoll Tuamotu, ringed with seventy palms.

The lifeless ropes of the raft creaked, and blond filaments stood up where the braids were torn. The logs, heavy with water, bobbed and slurped like dead things in the sea. Two sides of the bamboo cabin had blown away, its roof hung down like straw fallen from ricks. How bright, how clear the slow day and the sea.

Brave and bronze-chested, I pulled on the steering oar.

Weird. It was Audrey Meadows riding in the car with Dr. Epstein. She stepped out from the passenger side, and her lips were red as cardinal wings. She folded her proud arms and leaned against the car door. She glanced at Dr. Epstein, then scanned the yard. Her gaze stopped on me.

My Indian name is Caped Man with Coin Changer. I stood with the coin changer on my belt and Pookie's baton in my hand (which I twirled and dropped, twirled and dropped again). The towel cape was tied around my neck. Dr. Epstein walked up, looking, I thought, unusually tall. "I'm proud of you," he said.

"You should have seen Reba! She was a little teary. My wife wants to meet you, Aaron. It's been quite a day."

Audrey Meadows launched herself with one deft push of her hips and began to march toward me from the car. I backed up.

"And we're happy for your mother."

I clicked out a dime from the coin changer fast and put it back in its slot. I clicked out two nickels. Two more steps back.

Audrey Meadows reached me, bent over, and put her hands on her knees. I saw the shirred edge of her bra and a tiny pink bow between cups. "Hey, Aaron," she said. "Got change for a quarter?"

19

Behind the bearers, a train of pine torches pulsed in the night air. The tiger slowly swung on the poles. I followed them all from the thick woods on the narrow path to the village of Chowgarh and to the hut of the grieving woman. The dead girl's mother walked timidly to the door, and the tiger was lowered to the ground before her. She wept. She thanked me. Her feeble fingers raked my shirt, and she sang a Hindu prayer.

Mom said, "Mrs. Menard had a talk with Mrs. Warthead, and Kong is coming over to say he's sorry. Now, Aaron. Aaron? Look at me. When he comes, he's going to ask you to accept his apology. Just say yes, OK? Not a big deal. You don't have to discuss theories of childhood development or anything, just say yes. That's what nice people do. And that's all you have to say."

However and unfortunately, Kong Warthead stood in the forest with his foot in a bear trap. All the little chipmunks dived in there and chewed on his heel bones. (Kong went, "Huhn?")

I said, "Do we have to leave?"

Mom said, "Oh, you'll be fine. You'll have lots and lots of people to talk to. I'm going back to school in California. I'm going to get a job."

"No. I mean, I don't want to leave Pookie."

"You're not leaving Pookie."

"No. I mean, I don't want to leave the Swan, because . . ."

"You're not leaving the Swan, sweetheart. She goes away in winter like Persephone, and then she comes back."

"We won't know where the light switches are."

"We'll find the light switches."

"I won't be a Comet though."

"You'll be my comet."

"And I am here to tell you ... all the Chaldeans were greatly mystified ... and all the magicians and diviners and wise men and sorcerers were greatly mystified when Nebuchadnezzar addressed them. And he said, 'Who can interpret this dream?'

"Now, let us turn to number ten in the hymnal, 'Let All the World in Every Corner Sing.'"

20

Praised be the fathomless universe! And praised be Mom!

We drove west to Terre Haute and shot across the Wabash River, the mighty Wabash, and the waters stood like a heap. We flew like a rocket ship across Illinois, picked up Highway 66—

highway of Huckleberry Finn and Sal Paradise—and blazed like a meteor past fields of pale alfalfa, pale soybeans, past sun-skimmed pools of duckweed.

A breaking tidal air fell in the window and mussed my hair. I held tight to Pookie's baton and looked straight out the passenger window. The wilderness of Shur shuddered there like blurred boxcars.

Purple mountain majesties rolled toward us like knots on a capstan. Anacondas burped in the Amazon. Stormy South Pacific seas lay becalmed today, and the horned beaks of albatrosses smiled at Tuamotu. Cloud shadows ran through clattering Kansas corn while, aloft in prairie skies, Bridey Murphy flew, her red Irish hair streaming in dusk light, her white underpants illuminating whole districts of agricultural endeavor and export and also industry. Bridey pulled Jim Corbett—dazed by American light and blinking with joy—pulled Jim Corbett west with her right hand. The jet stream splayed his feet.

Bridey Murphy spoke to me. She said, "Don't fear dying, Aaron. You'll live to be an old man, and then you'll die, and then you'll come back a thousand times. You will sing in Estonian choirs, you will sway in salt swells in the Sea of Marmara, and you will sit on a rock in the jungles of Chowgarh with your Martini-Henry rifle across your knees, and smoke your pipe, and hear tigers growl in the bracken, and not fear a thing in the world."

Above Bridey, a choir of cherubs sang, knowing that the Feed the Jesus Fund was tucked away in the trunk of the car. Beside the Fund box lay a copy of Leonard Clark's *The Rivers Ran East,* and I'd find later on the flyleaf, "Have a good journey, Aaron! With love, Beatrice Menard."

Mom said, "You're going to be talking with Beverly on Santa Monica beaches in a couple of days. With Beverly and her new husband, Leslie Leopold."

On the horizon before us, the orange and most excellent sun so calm and haughty melted down. Behind us, everything I knew rolled away.

And poor hapless Pookie, my best fan in the world with her little trumpet, dreaming—I hoped—on the snows of Deneb, surrounded by horses, Pookie swung up with the night. Mom said I'd find her as easily from Santa Monica piers as from the backyards of Rocky Ripple, and right about now, in fact, in the northern sky, wheeling faster than any car could go, high over Meridian Street the Swan was rising.

Photo by Jason Madara

JIM COHEE was born in Bloomington, Indiana, during World War II. His father was a law student at IU, and the family lived at 800 East Atwater Avenue, walking distance from the Press. Jim's family moved briefly to Maryland after the war, then to Indianapolis. They lived in the Butler-Tarkington neighborhood there, a little south of the Rocky Ripple of the novel. Butler University was Jim's backyard. He visited his grandparents in Martinsville each summer and remembers its bricked streets and his grandmother's one-room schoolhouse. His great-great grandfather Noah Major is the author of an Indiana classic, *The Pioneers of Morgan County.*

The Cohee family left Indiana for California in 1957. Jim studied English literature and classical languages at UC Santa Barbara and San Francisco State University, then went into publishing. He edited trade books for twenty-five years for Sierra Club Books in San Francisco, working with Edward Abbey, Frederick Turner, and Rebecca Solnit, among others.

The Swan is Jim Cohee's first novel.

This book was designed by Jamison Cockerham and set in type by Tony Brewer at Indiana University Press and printed by Thomson-Shore, Inc.

The text type is Arno, designed by Robert Slimbach and issued by Adobe Systems, Inc. The display type is Emmascript, designed by Kanna Aoki and issued by MVB Fonts.